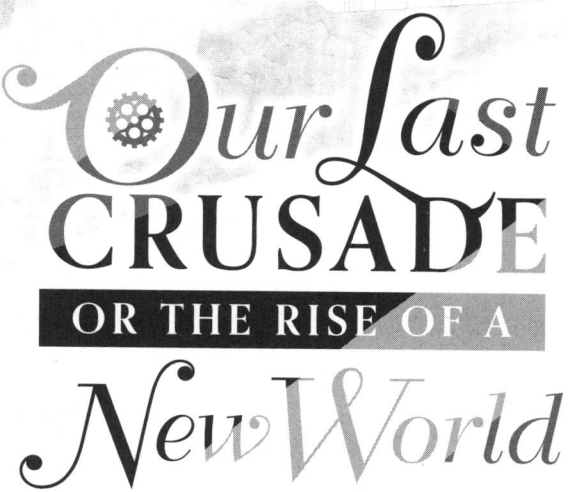

Our Last CRUSADE OR THE RISE OF A New World

11

KEI SAZANE

Illustration by
Ao Nekonabe

YEN ON

NEW YORK

11 KEI SAZANE

Translation by Jan Cash
Cover art by Ao Nekonabe

This book is a work of fiction. Names, characters, places, and incidents are the product of the author's imagination or are used fictitiously. Any resemblance to actual events, locales, or persons, living or dead, is coincidental.

KIMI TO BOKU NO SAIGO NO SENJO, ARUIWA SEKAI GA HAJIMARU SEISEN Vol. 11
©Kei Sazane, Ao Nekonabe 2021
First published in Japan in 2021 by KADOKAWA CORPORATION, Tokyo.
English translation rights arranged with KADOKAWA CORPORATION, Tokyo, through TUTTLE-MORI AGENCY, INC., Tokyo.

Yen On
150 West 30th Street, 19th Floor
New York, NY 10001

Visit us at yenpress.com
facebook.com/yenpress
twitter.com/yenpress
yenpress.tumblr.com
instagram.com/yenpress

First Yen On Edition: March 2023
Edited by Yen On Editorial: Shella Wu, Maya Deutsch
Designed by Yen Press Design: Liz Parlett

Yen On is an imprint of Yen Press, LLC.
The Yen On name and logo are trademarks of Yen Press, LLC.

The publisher is not responsible for websites (or their content) that are not owned by the publisher.

Cataloging in Publication data is on file with the Library of Congress.

ISBNs: 978-1-9753-4308-8 (paperback)
        978-1-9753-4309-5 (ebook)

10 9 8 7 6 5 4 3 2 1

LSC-C

Printed in the United States of America

Our Last
CRUSADE
OR THE RISE OF A
New World

"Just so you know in advance, the story you'll see is really a parting of ways."

Lord Yunmelngen
The symbol of the Empire and holds supreme authority. Invites Sisbell to the capital in order to learn the truth of the tragedy from a century ago.

Crossweil Gate Nebulis

A boy who came to the capital to work as a miner. He starts living with his distant relatives, the Nebulis twins.

Our Last Crusade or the Rise of a New World

Alicerose Sophi Nebulis
She has a meek personality and doesn't like conflict. She's the younger twin and her mature physique charms the men around her.

"Spend time with us."

"What are those two doing?"

Eve Sophi Nebulis
Cheerful and naive. Alicerose's older twin. Compared to her sister, she is childish and animated.

Yunmelngen
Because he can obtain anything he wants, he is very curious. He hopes the "new energy" will fix his weak constitution.

"We don't have a moment to spare."

Aliceliese Lou Nebulis IX
The second Nebulis princess. While she is without Rin, she heads as fast as she can to the Imperial capital to stop the awakened Founder.

"...So you just want me to show you what happened a century ago here?"

Sisbell Lou Nebulis IX
The third Nebulis princess. She is summoned by Lord Yunmelngen to the capital in order to recreate the events from a hundred years ago.

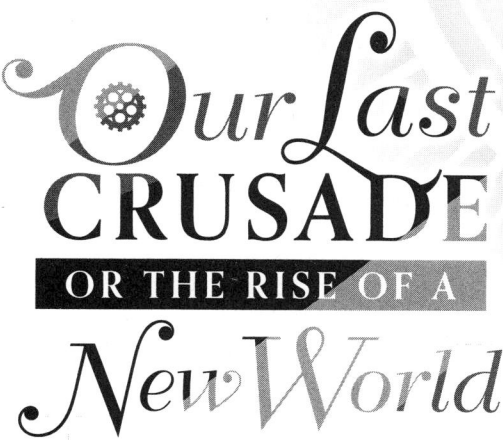

Our Last CRUSADE
OR THE RISE OF A
New World

So Se Iu, E nes siole Phi yumie.
The truly kind child.

hiz mis feo tis-kamyu Ec mihas, hiz kuo feo tis-emne Ec Ema,
Someone who remembers your pain and the one who inherits your will

rein hiz ole Ec et rein I rein.
shall dream of the imagined world you once dreamed of.

THE HEAVENLY EMPIRE

Iska

Member of Unit 907—Special Defense for Humankind, Third Division. Used to be the youngest soldier who ever reached the highest rank in the military, the Saint Disciples. Stripped of his title for helping a witch break out of prison. Wields a black astral sword to intercept astral power and its white counterpart to reproduce the last attack obstructed by its pair. An honest swordsman fighting for peace.

Mismis Klass

The commander of Unit 907. Baby-faced and often mistaken for a child, but actually a legal adult. Klutzy but responsible. Trusts her subordinates. Became a witch after plunging into a vortex.

Jhin Syulargun

The sniper of Unit 907. Prides himself on his deadly aim. Can't seem to shake off Iska, since they trained under the same mentor. Cool and sarcastic, though he has a soft spot for his buddies.

Nene Alkastone

Chief mechanic of Unit 907. Weapon-making genius. Mastered operation of a satellite that releases armor-piercing shots from a high altitude. Thinks of Iska as her older brother. Wide-eyed and loveable.

Risya In Empire

Saint Disciple of the fifth seat. Genius-of-all-trades. A beautiful woman often seen in a suit and glasses with dark green frames. Likes Mismis, her former classmate.

THE NEBULIS SOVEREIGNTY

Aliceliese Lou Nebulis IX

Second-born princess of Nebulis. Leading candidate for the next queen. Strongest astral mage, who attacks with ice. Feared by the Empire as the Ice Calamity Witch. Hates all the backstabbing happening in the Sovereignty. Enraptured by fair fights against Iska, an enemy swordsman she met on the battlefield.

Rin Vispose

Alice's attendant. An astral mage controlling earth. Maid uniform conceals weapons for assassination. Skilled at deadly espionage. Hard to read her expressions, but has an inferiority complex about her chest.

Sisbell Lou Nebulis IX

Youngest princess of Nebulis. Aliceliese's little sister. Possesses Illumination, which reproduces footage of past events. Saved by Iska when she was captured in the Empire.

Lord Mask On

A member of the House of Zoa, which directly competes with the princesses for the throne. A conspirator whose true motives are unclear.

Kissing Zoa Nebulis

A powerful astral mage. Called the favorite child of the Zoa. Possesses astral power of thorns.

Salinger

Strongest sorcerer. Imprisoned for attempting to assassinate the queen. Currently at large.

Elletear Lou Nebulis IX

Eldest princess of Nebulis. Focused on traveling abroad. Often absent from the palace.

Our Last CRUSADE OR THE RISE OF A New World

CONTENTS

SECRET

Iska, Still Unaware

"Wait! Master, I said wait!"

As he exhaled, his breath white, a black-haired boy named Iska chased after a man who was already leaving.

The terminal station of the continental railway was dyed in the colors of the sunset. As the travelers passed each other in the corridor, Iska couldn't catch up no matter how quickly he ran. He simply couldn't match the man's pace. Compared to the eleven-year-old boy, the man who he'd called "master" was over 1.8 meters tall.

"You always do stuff like this and leave me behind!"

"…" The man stopped in his tracks and whipped around. "Leave behind? Who leaves who behind?"

"You! *You* leave me behind!"

"…"

"You haven't noticed?"

"I was just lost in my thoughts," the man replied.

The boy sighed. Iska slumped his shoulders when his teacher showed no admission of wrongdoing. This was how he always acted.

His master was a carefree wanderer who always had his head in the clouds. And whenever Iska thought the man was going to tell him something meaningful, he would always receive some half-baked response instead.

But this man was also the strongest swordsman in the Empire.

Crossweil Nes Lebeaxgate. He stood there, his long coat covering his slim figure—not a single bit of excess fat on him. In the past, when he had led the Saint Disciples, his moniker had been the Black Steel Gladiator, but he rarely spoke of those times now. According to the man himself, it wasn't that he was reluctant to talk about that period in his life so much as he simply couldn't be bothered.

"The special express train will soon be departing for Vale Republic. Ticketholders are advised to board as they wait for departure."

"Say, master?" As Iska listened to the announcement, he looked up at the man. "Why are we getting on a train?"

Iska still had no idea whether they were heading out for vacation or a tour of duty. He was suddenly told the day before that they would be going on a trip, which he'd been fine preparing for, but he still had yet to learn what his master was hoping to accomplish—as per usual.

"What are we going to do once we leave the Empire?" he asked.

"We're going to learn what it's like outside," Crossweil replied simply.

"What good does knowing that do?"

"…"

The strongest swordsman in the Empire looked up at the station's ceiling.

"We're doing this because you have yet to learn what a witch really is," he said.

SECRET

"…I know a little bit," Iska countered.

There likely wasn't a single person in the Empire who didn't know what a witch was. They were former humans who had been possessed by the inexplicable energy known as astral power. Witches were terrifying beings and were capable of using astral power as they desired. They were wicked, aggressive, and loathed the Empire.

Such was Iska's impression.

Now, this was only his impression because Iska had never spoken to a witch himself. He had learned everything he knew of them through word of mouth.

"I wouldn't say that you've got the wrong idea about witches," the man said, "but that isn't all there is to them."

His teacher looked around at the people heading here and there throughout the station.

"The stories passed down in the Empire about witches only apply to a minority—with exceptions like the Grand Witch Nebulis. Ninety percent of witches aren't much different from your average human. Iska, what do you think of the people walking around in this station?"

"They look like normal people to me…"

He saw businessmen boarding their trains and families on outings. They all looked like ordinary people to him.

"It's highly likely there may be witches and sorcerers among them. But they all look exactly the same as any Imperial. Do any of them seem wicked to you?"

"No."

"So, this is just as true as all the other stories told in the Empire. Everything you're taking in with your eyes right now is real. You'll do well to keep both sides in mind."

"……Got it."

Iska was lying. He really didn't get it. After all, as far as he was concerned, witches were frightening.

Of course, he tried his best to take in his master's teachings, but Iska still couldn't toss the preconceptions he'd developed from being born and raised in the empire aside.

"You'll learn eventually," the man said. "That's the whole reason we've traveled out this far."

"......Yes, sir."

As for his teacher's true intentions...

Iska would not see and understand those for himself until many years later.

PROLOGUE

What Alice Desires

"Founder."

"You intend to burn down the Empire, do you not?"

She had been too late—for everything.

Alice felt dizzy, panting heavily as she cut through the first-floor hall of the Nebulis palace and dashed into the courtyard.

"Shuvalts!"

"Lady Alice, this way!"

Waiting for her was the palatial custom-made car, Cadillac One.

Shuvalts, an attendant dressed in a formal suit, held the door open for Alice as she arrived. He had served both the House of Lou and Alice's younger sister, Sisbell, for many years.

Though at present, he was temporarily waiting on Alice instead.

Alice had no attendant.

And Shuvalts had no lady to serve.

Both Rin and Sisbell, the people who normally fulfilled those roles, were in the Imperial capital, Yunmelngen.

Alice was leaving the Sovereignty with the sole goal of saving the two.

However...

This time she was not rescuing them from the clutches of Imperial soldiers. But she *was* rushing to their aid to save them from the Founder Nebulis herself before the Empire was razed to the ground.

"I've informed Her Majesty. Quickly, now!"

"Yes, without delay," Shuvalts replied.

No sooner was Alice seated in the vehicle than it whisked her out of the courtyard at breakneck speed.

"I shall take you to Zahl International Airport," the attendant informed her. "A private plane will bring you to a country neighboring the Empire, after which you will travel by railway to the border."

"Yes, thank you. Any method of travel will do, so long as it gets me there the fastest."

"That is what I had hoped to arrange...however...," Shuvalts spoke to her from the driver's seat. His stifled voice was filled with deep concern and worry. "...it seems the Revered Founder has awakened."

"Yes, some hours ago. She disappeared right before my very eyes."

She reclined deep into her seat, her hands clenched tightly into fists over her lap.

"The Grand Witch plans to burn the Empire to the ground," Alice continued. "She doesn't care who stands in her way. Even her own kindred."

"Are you planning on destroying the Empire...?"
"What else is there for me to do?"

*　　*　　*

She planned to leave a scorched trail behind her as she merci-lessly approached the Empire.

...This is serious.

...Rin is imprisoned in the Imperial capital and Iska is there, too!

And other Sovereign people. They had many spies within the Empire collecting intelligence. The Founder would likely spare them no mercy as she burned the entire city to the ground.

"You do not need to call her 'revered' anymore," Alice said. "We shouldn't worship that Grand Witch any longer. She's a calamity, a being that only wishes for destruction."

"I can hardly believe it," Shuvalts said, his voice sounding heavy—which of course it would.

To all the Sovereignty's mages, the Founder Nebulis was the symbol of hope who guided them. Alice hadn't so much as questioned the dogma herself in the past, and she could hardly think the queen had, either. But it seemed that their beliefs were far off the mark.

The witch was willing to sacrifice her own people solely for the sake of destroying the Empire.

"If she attacks them, Rin and Sisbell will be caught in the crossfire. And that's not all. Though the Empire has done their fair share of damage, we would end up in an all-out war with them as well."

The Heavenly Empire and Nebulis Sovereignty.

Though the two superpowers had clashed in proxy skirmishes around the world, they had historically been able to avoid a full-scale war. If that were to happen, the countries bordering them would be dragged into the mire as well. It would lead to total world destruction. Alice needed to avoid that at all costs.

"We must be careful, Shuvalts. The steps we take now will create large ripples throughout the world. If we can't stop the Founder, it's the end of everything."

"...I will bear that in mind," the attendant replied.

"According to Her Majesty, the Founder disappeared after floating above the palace. She left for the Empire using some type of space-time astral power."

And the two of them were pursuing her now.

...She can teleport. She's faster than any plane.

...No matter how much I hurry, it'll take me a full day to arrive at the Empire's border.

Ironically, she could only hope that the Imperial forces would be able to hold back the Founder during that time. To make matters worse, Alice could not dedicate herself entirely to stopping the Founder. Much to her consternation, there was another issue she had to attend to as well.

"It seems the Hydra have yet to mobilize."

Shuvalts stole a glance, staring into her eyes through the rearview mirror.

"They are under Her Majesty's watchful gaze. Her elite guards are keeping a close eye on them, as they were behind Lady Sisbell's kidnapping," Shuvalts said. "Not a single one of them has left the Sun Spire. Not their leader, Talisman, or even Princess Mizerhyby."

"...I do wonder if they simply do not care."

The Hydra's goal was to win the conclave. Their primary objective was to obtain the throne and choose the next queen, so the chaos the Founder or the Imperial forces caused was likely of little concern to them. In fact, they probably hoped the Founder and the Empire would annihilate each other.

"We can leave the Hydra to Her Majesty," Alice said. "Our real trouble will be the Zoa."

Yes. Lord Mask and the entire Zoa family, who had Kissing on their side, would cause the most trouble.

… The Zoa's greatest wish is to destroy the Empire.

… The Founder's awakening is the opportunity of a lifetime for them.

And they had taken the initiative with that.

"Her Majesty just informed me that Lord Mask and Kissing did not appear at the meeting, even though they were supposedly in the Moon Spire."

They must have left the palace to follow the Founder.

The Zoa had departed to take advantage of the Grand Witch's thirst for revenge, apparently to save their head of house Growley, who had been captured by the Imperial forces—but that was only a pretense to start an all-out war.

"Do you wish for an all-out war with the Empire?"

"Of course. That is the greatest desire of all mages for the last century."

They would be arriving at the Empire in the order in which they left. The Revered Founder would likely be the fastest, then Lord Mask and Kissing would probably follow, and Alice would be there last.

"We must hurry, Shuvalts," she urged.

She wasn't trying to remind him. Instead, Alice was saying that for herself, repeating it to herself again.

"We don't have a moment to spare."

CHAPTER 1

The Planet Keeps a Memory

1

The largest city in the world, the Imperial capital, Yunmelngen.

The city was divided into three sectors. The first was where the government and research facilities were gathered. The assembly would convene there and use its full authority to decide all political matters of the Empire.

The second sector was the residential district. Seventy percent of the Imperial capital's populace lived there. Next door was the world-leading business district that tourists all over the world visited.

Then there was the third...

It was the permanent residence of the Imperial forces and had numerous magnificent training grounds.

"So we've finally made it to the capital..."

They were in front of a vacant lot in Sector Two. Sisbell looked up at the sky after getting out of the car. It was already the middle of the night. The sun had set beyond the horizon and the faint gloom of the clouds expanded.

It wasn't pitch-black. Despite it being the middle of the night, the sky above the Imperial capital was bright.

"It's too bright for nighttime...it makes me feel uneasy." Sisbell seemed somewhat exasperated as she sighed. "The light from the buildings of the business district is so radiant that I can't even see the glow of the stars. It would be hard believe it if it were the Sovereignty."

"Shh, they'll be able to hear, Miss Sisbell," Commander Mismis whispered in a panic.

This was the worst place in the world a witch could be. Had anyone heard Sisbell, the military police likely would have forced their way over from anywhere.

"Hey, Jhin Big Bro, we've finally made it home, haven't we?"

"Home is still home, no longer how long it's been."

"But I'm not sure I'm happy about it...," Nene said. "I think I'm more nervous."

"We've got a huge job ahead of us, that's for sure."

Jhin and Nene were both looking up ahead at the checkpoint.

"Okay, everyone get in. You're driving, Nene." Risya waved them over from inside the car.

Her face was covered in bandages; they also wrapped around her thigh over what appeared to be a painful wound. It was the aftermath of the fight with Luclezeus, one of the Eight Great Apostles.

On the way over to the capital, instead of finding Lord Yunmelngen waiting for them, they'd gotten caught in a trap set by the Apostles. The Empire was no monolith. The Apostles had been waiting vigilantly for an opportunity to strike against Lord Yunmelngen.

...Luclezeus's cyberbrain is gone.

...We've unquestionably cut ties with the Apostles after that battle.

They couldn't let their guard down in the capital.

Assassins under the employ of the Apostles could strike at any moment.

"Oh, little Nene, you know where Castle Tower Seat is, don't you?"

"Y-yes...," Nene answered.

"Then off we go!" Risya proclaimed. "Can't keep Their Excellency waiting."

The car drove off. Unit 907, Sisbell, and Risya, the Lord's staff officer, headed toward the Lord's residence.

"Hey, Isk?" Risya, who sat across from Iska, looked at him. "What's wrong? Why the glum face?"

"...I think you could make a guess," Iska answered.

"Because of all the trouble that's going to come from picking a fight with the Apostles?"

"There's that too," he responded.

"Then is it nerves from having an audience with the Their Excellency?"

"That's another reason."

But he had been prepared for both of those things. In actuality, the one thing he wasn't internally prepared for was something else entirely...

"Are you really that surprised I returned to the capital?"

It was his master—the black-haired man dressed in matching black garb. He couldn't wipe the image from his mind.

"...I wasn't expecting to see him so soon," Iska said.

"You mean the man you served under, Isk?"

"I didn't serve him—he was my teacher."

The Black Steel Gladiator, Crossweil.

He was the Lord's former guard and the first owner of the astral swords. He had wandered throughout the Empire, finding and training youth with promise. Iska and Jhin were the only pupils of his who had endured his agonizing training to the end. After giving Jhin a specialized sniper rifle, and Iska the astral swords, their teacher abruptly went into hiding.

"He left us and disappeared," Iska said. "I can see how we could run into him by chance. But I didn't think he'd appear at a time like this…"

"If you're going to go see Yunmelngen, you ought to hurry."

It had been too sudden.

The moment they met, he had told them to go see the Lord. Not only that, his master had addressed the ruler of the Empire so casually, which took Iska aback.

…Risya, his staff officer, calls the Lord "Their Excellency."

…But my master doesn't.

He said Yunmelngen. Almost as though the Lord was a personal acquaintance.

"Do you know anything about it, Risya?"

"Hmm…just that it's complicated between them," she replied. "If you're that curious, why don't you ask Their Excellency himself?"

There Risya was, saying that as though it was obvious. She turned to look out the window of the car as though something had suddenly occurred to her.

"Right on time. Nene, turn there and pull over."

They had arrived at a gigantic building that towered over its surroundings. Castle Tower Seat, also sometimes referred to as the "windowless building."

2

The Castle Tower Seat.

It was the last building left after the Founder Nebulis's destruction a century ago.

"This is the only place I can't get into based on recognition alone," Risya said as she got out of the car.

The ID card she had produced used cutting-edge technology for authentication. Even the staff officer to the Lord herself wasn't allowed to come and go as she pleased without verifying who she was.

"Risya In Empire, entry approved."

"Thank you very much."

Risya headed back into the car.

"Nene, you can drive in," Risya said. "Head straight to the facility."

"I can feel the years being shaved off my life...," Sisbell, who had been holding her breath until that very moment, replied in Nene's place. "What if they ask to see inside the car?"

"Just pretend you don't know anything. You'll be fine—as long as you don't accidentally let slip that you're the Third Princess of the Nebulis Sovereignty, that is. That's the whole point of why I've come here with you."

"But what happens if the guards inside overhear?"

"Oh, no, that's not how it works. You can talk freely inside."

"What?"

"The whole place is unmanned," Risya said, gesturing toward the reddish-brown building with her chin.

"The Lord's residence is empty. I mean, you've seen what Their Excellency looks like."

Inside Castle Tower Seat, Sisbell widened her eyes at the sight that greeted her.

"How is it so quiet?"

It was deserted. Although there were security cameras dotting the ceiling, the hallway stretching tens of meters in front of them was empty. Not a single person was walking through it.

Clack…clack…

Only their footfalls echoed through the hall. They saw neither guards nor office workers.

"Is this what you meant earlier? Risya, or whatever your name is."

"There are people around. Iska should know. A Saint Disciple permanently stationed here, actually. It's just that we hardly ever bump into each other in a place as big as this."

"I'm surprised you consider this to be good security."

"Do you really think there's anyone out there who would attempt something?"

Risya, who had been at the front, turned around to shrug at Sisbell.

"Who on earth do you think would sneak into the Lord's residence, which is in the middle of the capital, escape past the Saint Disciple, and try to go after the life of Their Excellency?"

"…"

"That's the whole reason why we keep this place a secret from you, Princess Sisbell, and the rest of the people of the Sovereignty."

"…I'm not sure how to feel about all of this," Sisbell said.

"Anyway, we're almost there," Risya stated.

The Castle Tower Seat was split into five parts. The gigantic building had four towers and glass corridors that led deeper inside. The fifth building was the Heaven Between Insight and Nosight. A lone black pedestal stood in front of its entrance.

"'Heaven above, heaven below, honor only to the emperor'... oops. Princess Sisbell, bear in mind that the code to open these doors is also a secret. Only about thirty people in the entire Empire know it."

Risya smirked as the doors opened in front of her to a crimson reception hall. It looked out of place in the building, which had seemed so lifeless until now.

The soft scent of wooden boards and the sharp prickle of rush grasses hit their nostrils. The dazzling vermillion interior felt almost otherworldly, like it had come from a different place entirely.

And deeper in the room...

"Hey there. Finally made it, have you?"

A silver-furred beastperson was lying on top of tatami mats. Their face looked like a cross between a cat's and a human girl's. Their eyes were large like a kitten's and seemed almost friendly.

A beastperson.

Though they looked like a monster on the outside, this beastperson held the highest authority in the Empire: Lord Yunmelngen.

"I was getting so tired of waiting for you. She was, too."

"Rin!"

There was a pillar behind the Lord. When Sisbell shouted, everyone stared at it. A brown-haired girl was tied to it. Her arms and legs were bound by ropes of straw as thick as a person's wrists.

"...Lady Sisbell...I'm so sorry..." Rin gritted her teeth. "To think I could let you see me in such a sorry state after being captured by the enemy… This is my life's greatest failure…"

"Rin! I'll save you right now!" Sisbell pointed a finger at the Lord with determination. "Release Rin! I came here, just like you wanted. So set your hostage free like you promised."

"All right," the Lord said.

"I see. You have no intention to. Well, I'm going to give you a piece of my…… Wait, what?"

"I just said she can go. You're a very bad listener." The Lord yawned. **"And just so you know, I haven't been keeping Rin tied up. She's been free to do as she pleases."**

"……Come again?" Sisbell was taken aback. She blinked. "What in the world do you mean?"

"Rin tied herself to this pillar. She said it wouldn't have looked good for her to have been wandering about this whole time, so she opted to bind herself before you got here. This was all her doing."

"Y-you dummy!" Rin shouted. "I told you not to tell them… ugh, really!"

The ropes around her unraveled. They hadn't been tied tightly from the start. Just the slightest tug had been enough to pull her free. It was apparent to Iska the moment he saw it.

…Jhin, Nene, Commander Mismis, and Risya of course must have also realized.

…Sisbell was the only one to fall for it.

The princess looked dumbfounded.

After freeing herself, Rin knelt on a knee in front of the princess and lowered her head.

"It's as you see, Lady Sisbell."

"…So this farce was your idea? I feel like you deserve more of a scolding than the Lord right now."

"It is as you see," Rin repeated, her head still bowed. "The Lord did not show any sign they were going to hurt me in any way. Much as I detest this beast for leading the Empire, I believe they will not harm you either, Lady Sisbell."

"I'm pretty sure I told you that from the start."

The Lord slowly started to move. They leisurely pulled themself up to sit straight.

"Third Princess of the Nebulis Sovereignty."

"Wh-what is it..."

"There's no need to be frightened. You came here prepared, didn't you?"

"...Prepared for what?"

"Prepared to see the worst day in the world."

The silver beastperson rose to their feet. They looked at Sisbell, then Iska and the rest of the unit, and Risya.

"Come with me," they said.

3

The continental railroad runs north to south through the land.

An express train, speeding straight through the reddish-brown terrain of the wastelands.

"..."

The black-haired girl held the windowsill as she stared at the scenery.

She was likely thirteen, maybe fourteen. Her hair had a beautiful sheen to it, and the dress she wore was dazzling in its own way. Adorable as she was, she gave off a doll-like impression.

Though her eyes were covered...

She had been staring at the scenery from the train for over an hour.

"Do you find it unusual, Kissing?" A man in black wearing a metal mask sat across from her. He was Lord Mask On Zoa Nebulis, the proxy head of the Zoa family, and she was the Zoa's candidate for queen.

"Come to think of it, this is your first time on a train, isn't it?" he remarked.

"...Yes, dearest Uncle." She nodded.

Lord Mask stopped her from turning back around.

"No, you may keep looking. It is your first time seeing this place, after all. You should enjoy the scenery."

"...Dearest Uncle, what is that city?"

Kissing pointed toward the horizon. Far off into the reddish-brown terrain, faint buildings that did indeed look like a city peeked over the skyline.

"The neutral city Ain. A place where culture and the arts flourish," Lord Mask explained.

"...Culture and the arts?"

"Yes. But I cannot recommend going there. We are right on the edge of Imperial territory. You may run into Imperial soldiers who are on leave in that area."

"I would eliminate them if I did," the girl replied.

"We can avoid all of that trouble," the man told her. "From here, we are striking at the source itself."

The Imperial territory and the Imperial capital Yunmelngen would be on the receiving end of an attack soon enough. Though only members of the Zoa's personal soldiers were on the train, they were elite forces under Kissing's direct command.

"The clash between the Revered Founder and Imperial forces will commence. They will likely dedicate all their efforts to stopping the Founder. And during that time, we will invade the Imperial capital."

".......Yes."

"The queen has likely caught wind of our movements by now," Lord Mask continued. "I wonder who will come to stop us... Yes, I believe dear Alice would follow close behind. She must be quite livid as well."

The Lous would never endorse a war with the Empire. They would undoubtedly come to stop the Founder and the Zoas.

"But you are too late," Lord Mask said.

They would never make it in time if they left the Sovereignty now.

"You would do better to go back, dearest Alice. You would never be able to stop the Revered Founder, no matter how hard you try. Once you arrive, all you will see is the charred wastelands of what was once called the Empire."

Elevation: 10,000 meters.

The space was filled with a great sea of clouds, fluffy as cotton and vast as a mountain. A gigantic aircraft flew across the grandiose vista. The Nebulis royalty's private jet was outfitted with a changing room specially for the royal family's use. And in that suite...

"Lady Alice, I have prepared them for you."

".......Yes. Thank you," Alice said, wearing nothing but her undergarments.

An attendant was carefully covering Alice's fully exposed back with self-adhesives to hide the wing-like astral crest on Alice's back.

She felt a cold sting with every new adhesive. Each one felt the same as a cold compress touching her skin. For Alice, the experience was akin to being given a shot as a child—a thing to be endured. Her astral crest was much larger than others, more than either of her siblings' or her mother's. It may have been the largest in the royal family.

The only person who could possibly have a comparable one was...

...*The Founder.*

...*Her crest has the same wing shape as mine, and it's large enough to nearly cover her back.*

There was some correlation between one's crest and astral power. There were cases of mages with small astral crests having powerful abilities, but almost none to speak of when it came to the opposite.

...*My astral crest is my pride and joy. It's proof I am an astral mage.*

...*How ironic that I'll need to do everything in my power to stop someone with a crest that most looks like mine.*

"Your royal garments," the attendant said.

"Thank you."

Alice put on the clothes that were handed to her. Normally, Rin would be by her side, deftly aiding her. Just this once, however, she clumsily dressed herself alone.

"A message from Her Majesty," the attendant stated from beside Alice.

The Lou attendant's voice was soft as she continued, "A man we believe to be Lord Mask has been witnessed boarding a train to the Empire. Several members of the Zoa household are accompanying him."

"Where is the train headed?"

"We believe they will arrive at the Imperial border in four to five hours."

"...I see."

She gritted her teeth.

Indeed, they were a step ahead. Though the Zoa had completed their air travel and were already boarding a train, Alice herself was still in the air.

...And it's not just the Zoa.

...The Founder will have already arrived at the Empire as well. Conflict could break out at any moment.

This was no laughing matter.

Alice couldn't let the Empire, Rin, or Sisbell to be caught in the crossfire. And...

"I've had enough of this. Founder or not, I won't forgive her if she lays a hand on my Iska."

"Lady Alice?"

"Oh. I–it's nothing at all!"

She'd gotten so lost in her own anger that she'd said that aloud.

Alice waved her hands in a panic as the attendant looked at her face quizzically.

"...Just talking to myself."

The faraway Empire. The place that she should have detested most in this world now brought up a turmoil of complicated feelings inside her.

4

The Castle Tower Seat.

Everyone followed after Lord Yunmelngen onto an elevator that was directly connected to their chambers.

They went down, down, down.

Down to the underground level.

No. Not a level, but into the depths of the planet itself.

The elevator display didn't show labels such as "Underground 1" or "Underground 2." Instead, it displayed exactly how far they were below the surface of the earth—over four hundred meters at present.

"...Where do you intend on taking us?" Sisbell asked.

"Hm?"

The Lord, who stood at the center of the elevator, turned to look at Sisbell.

"I'm afraid this is the only way, Princess Sisbell. Your astral power has a limited scope when you view the past. I believe you said it was within three thousand meters of you."

"...But just how far underground are you going to take us?"

"I would like to see what occurred in the past about five thousand meters underground. So that means your ability won't work until we get to the two-thousand-meter mark. Looks like we've arrived."

They were now two thousand meters underground. The elevator opened to a gloomy and large empty hall.

"Oh? A room directly beneath the Lord's residence? I think this is my first time here as well." Risya looked around curiously.

Ahead of them, Lord Yunmelngen sauntered into the center of the hall.

"Well, here we are. Princess Sisbell, I'm sure you know what to do."

"...So you just want me to show you what happened a century ago here?" she asked.

"Yes, that's all there is to it."

The silver beastperson turned around.

"The birth of the Founder Nebulis. Of me. Of the Black Steel Gladiator, Crossweil. And the story of how the astral swords were created. I want to see all of it."

"..." Sisbell inhaled deeply. She unbuttoned her bodice and

pulled away the self-adhesive under her collarbone, exposing her astral crest.

The Illumination astral power. The crest—proof she was a witch—at first faint, soon began to glow more intensely.

"There's something I'd like to know first. With the Illumination astral power, do you want me to show you everything from a century ago without any filters? If you can tell me the exact people and places you want to see, that should make things go more efficiently."

"Ah, I see," the Lord said. "Then you can focus on me and—"

They stopped themselves and snapped their fingers.

"Right. I know just the perfect person. You all saw Crow, didn't you? I can still smell him on you."

"...? We saw whom?" Sisbell froze and opened her eyes wide as saucers. Of course the Nebulis princess wouldn't know who Crow was.

And so...

"He means Crossweil," Iska said so Sisbell would also understand. "We just saw him. He's my teacher, and Jhin's too."

"Yes, he must have come out of the woodwork for this. He's just telling us to look at his past. We'll be able to find out everything by following it. However..."

The Lord's tone grew anxious.

The silver-haired beast continued, "Just so you know in advance, what you see here won't be an easy watch or anything of the sort. The story you'll see is really a parting of ways."

The hall was enveloped in light.

The glitter from Sisbell's astral power created three-dimensional images.

She had re-created the Empire of a century ago.

MEMORY ILLUMINATION 1

The Sisters and the Eccentric

1

The united stronghold, the Heavenly Empire.

This country, also commonly referred to as the Empire, was bolstered by the deposits of iron ore and rare metals that were being found in large quantities. Through its discoveries, its people created advanced machinery.

They forged ahead with machinery, improving their residences, and even their weaponry. They could create all manners of things, with iron at their core from their vast reserves of metals. And so, there was a demand for workers in the Empire.

They gathered youths from all over the world to mine their very many resources. At the time, Iska's teacher Crossweil Gate Nebulis was just a tender fifteen-year-old who had arrived at the Empire among the other immigrants.

2

The Imperial capital, Harkenweltz.

Eleventh Avenue, an area of many multi-tenant buildings.

The large street was littered with a mix of residences made of wood, prefab constructions made from flimsy steel, and even brand-new steel-framed buildings. In one corner of the road, the young black-haired Crossweil held a map in his hand as he walked.

…*Plit.*

Something felt sticky on the sole of his shoe—he must have stepped in some discarded gum. Or perhaps some paint or furniture glue? He couldn't tell, which only showed how chaotic the main thoroughfare was, especially with the crowds and clamor common all over the Imperial capital.

"…And the smell of the smoke."

He could trace its origin to the smokestacks of the factories. They were quite literally everywhere as they were needed to process the iron extracted from the ground, so the smell of chemicals and smoke was thick in the air.

"I knew it would be like this, but is this dirty town really going to become my home?…"

He adjusted his backpack and continued on.

His destination was the residential district. He wasn't heading to any of the large estates or luxury condos. The neighborhood was filled with prefab houses—the type that could have been constructed overnight if needed. This was the gathering place, and temporary residence, of the young hopefuls who had traveled to the Empire for work. And once he was in the right area…

He found the house that he would be staying at to be mind-boggling—in a bad way.

"...What kind of rubbish heap of a house is this?"

The prefab structure was simple—in the sense that they had done nothing but bend flimsy sheets of metal to construct it. In fact, it was made of a single sheet of metal. The walls were discolored with rust from being exposed to the elements.

"Can you really call this a house? It looks more like a shed or a storage place. I feel like I could find a nicer doghouse in the countryside..."

From this day forward, this would be his home.

He hesitantly knocked on the door, still struggling to accept his reality. He received an answer immediately:

"Nobody's home."

"......Huh?"

"No one's here."

It was a young girl's voice. Though her voice sounded sweet, it was also sharp, and she did not hide her annoyance.

"Oh, come on! There's definitely someone here! You just answered me!" He knocked once more. This time he pounded on it with his fist. "Come on, open up!"

"Nobody's home."

"Liar!"

"If you're here for the bills, our paycheck comes in five days, so come back then. If you're here to sell something, we haven't got the money to buy anything, but you can come back in ten years."

"No, I'm not..."

"Oh, shut up!"

The door burst open.

A girl with tan skin and straw-colored hair had kicked open the door with the force of a rocket, and her blows were hurtling at his face with the same momentum.

"Gah!"

Crossweil collapsed as she sent a barrage of kicks into him. The girl, who had landed straddling his face, was looking down at him. She cocked her head to the side quizzically.

"Hm? I feel like I've seen you before."

"…"

She had beat him so thoroughly that he was still writhing in agony.

She stared him in the face.

"Oh, it's just you, Crow." The tan girl started to laugh.

Eve Sofi Nebulis. His fifteen-year-old, distantly related adoptive sister hadn't changed in looks or personality since he'd last seen her two years ago.

"Really brings me back. You're so lanky, but you've gotten bigger. When we used to take baths together, you'd run away because you didn't like the shampoo."

"…My nose hurts" was his only reply.

"Well, good job finding your way here. The roads in the capital are so messed up, you almost got lost, am I right?" Eve cackled. "Well, looks like it's the three of us starting today. Let's make this fun, shall we?"

The junk house (according to Crossweil, at least).

Eve invited him in.

"…It still hurts."

"Ah-ha-ha, don't be so mad. Your nose just had a reunion with my knee, is all."

"Guess all my memories of you being nice were fake…"

"I *am* nice. Here, have some water."

Wouldn't one normally serve tea in this situation?

But Crossweil stopped himself from making that quip. They didn't have luxuries like tea. Coffee was also out of the question. It was plain as day when he saw the inside.

"Uh…"

The cup Eve thrust at him was on the ground.

"You don't even have a table?" he asked.

"That would just get in the way of sleeping. The room's small enough as it is."

He sat on the floor, which was bereft of even a cushion for guests. It was hard and cold. There was no furniture to speak of except a washing machine and fridge. No tables, no shelves. Since the space also lacked a closet, the occupants' clothes were neatly folded and laid in a corner. As a maturing lad, Crossweil had a hard time figuring out where to direct his gaze when he spotted what looked like undergarments. Eve herself, on the other hand, didn't seem concerned in the slightest.

"Well, this is pretty normal for the young people coming to the Empire for work."

"I thought the Empire would be a little more glamorous."

"You have to be above middle class for that," she told him, not missing a beat. "But we do make a lot more as miners here than we would in any other country. That's the whole reason why we came to work in the Empire, and why you made your way here, after all."

"But if the pay is so good, what's up with this house?"

"We send half our pay home each month. What's so bad about it, though? Living in a run-down place like this can be fun in its own way. Oh, right, so about the work." Eve clapped her hands together.

She made her way over to a corner of the room where there was a pile of food and other junk. After pushing her way through the mountain of things, she produced an electric saw and nail gun.

"There you go."

"…What?"

After thrusting the appliances at him, she pointed up at the ceiling, again without missing a beat.

"We've had leaks recently. Ahh, I sure am glad we've got another set of hands to help out now."

"Could I head back home…?"

The largest nation in the world, with beautiful city streets, was a civilization with dazzling sophisticated machinery. It was the best place in the world for young people to find employment.

So he had been taught and so he had believed.

The youth all over the world likely believed in that image of the Empire.

"It was all a lie…"

Those actually enjoying the prosperity of the Empire were in the middle class and above. The lower stratum, which comprised about forty percent of the population, lived to work and had nothing to show for it but frugal prefab abodes.

"I came here to make more money. I can't believe we're living somewhere smaller and more run-down than back home."

He looked up at the clear gray sky. Though that seemed contradictory, he didn't know how to describe it otherwise. It was both of those things. Because of the eternally spewing smoke from the factories, the sky was a constant gloomy shade.

"The toxins in the smoke rise and come down with the rain. So we really need to patch those leaks...there."

They were hammering down metal plates over a large hole in the roof. Ultimately, it was just a stopgap solution. Even though they'd covered the hole, the acid rain would still continue and corrode the metal—he was sure of it.

"Oh? Is that...?" A voice came from the entryway.

A girl holding a supermarket bag looked up and, upon catching sight of him, beamed.

"I knew it was you, Crow! I knew you'd be here any minute!"

She waved a hand dramatically at him.

"It's been so long," she continued. "You've gotten so big!"

"Alice! It has been too long."

Alicerose Sofi Nebulis—Crossweil's other adoptive sister. Eve and Alicerose were twins, and Eve was the older of the two. He remembered them looking exactly alike, both in features and in stature, but...

"...? What's wrong, Crow?"

"Uh...no, it's just um..."

He got down from the roof and faced Alicerose. The girl in front of him had grown up in the last two years, maturing into a lovely adult. Her dazzling golden hair was silky as it fluttered in the wind, and her ruby eyes were imposing and dignified. Her sculpted profile and blood-red lips were elegant and alluring.

Then there was her figure. The swell of her developed chest under her dress was far from what could be called underdeveloped. To be blunt, she didn't seem like she could possibly be Eve's twin, much less her younger sister.

"Uh, are you sure you weren't the older one, Alice? And that Eve is the younger one."

"Huh? Oh, Crow, what are you talking about," Alicerose laughed in response.

"Eve will be mad if she hears that, you know. She's already—"

"I HEARD that."

The door burst open, and the other sister poked her head out.

"You, Crow!" Eve stood next to Alicerose. "That's not the reaction I got when you first saw me. Why're you acting so giddy to see Alice?"

"Huh? Uh, I think you've got the wrong idea...actually I seem to recall you greeting me with a kick straight to the head when we met. Of course I acted differently."

"Shut up! I'm the older one here. You'd better show me some respect!" Eve shouted, placing a hand on her hip.

Out of the two twins, Eve hadn't grown significantly in the past two years, while Alicerose had matured so much she looked like she was the older one.

"Sheesh. So what if I'm short and look more like a kid?" She pouted sulkily. That made her seem more childlike, but if he told her that, he knew she would be even more upset.

"Eve, you can't put Crow on the spot like that..."

"This is all your fault!"

"Eep! Wh-what are you doing, Eve?!"

Eve had latched on to Alicerose's back—and had just so happened to grab on to her sister's voluptuous breasts to stabilize herself.

"What are these?! What are these giant things I'm holding? I bet they're sucking up all the nourishment that's supposed to be going toward *my* growth!"

"E-Eve?!" Alicerose turned bright red from being groped. "Y-you need to stop...Crow can see!"

"You're the one showing them off! Everybody calls me a terrible older sister. They think I'm underdeveloped because of you!"

"S-stop…please, Eve!"

They weren't hiding their fight at all.

"Looks like you two are living it up…," Crossweil said in a monotone.

This was the start to their life together in the Imperial capital.

3

In the Imperial capital of Harkenweltz, there were plenty of jobs to be found.

One of which was digging for the abundance of iron ore and rare metals directly below the capital. The Imperials were not the only ones mining. Migrants from all over the world had gathered for the job.

"Welcome to the fifty-fourth excavation point."

This was the mining grounds.

A man in a worker's uniform raised his voice in front of Crossweil and the other fresh recruits.

"I am the site foreman, Lavitch von Grehaim. I used to be a day laborer just like you, but my work was appreciated by the capital officials, and I clawed my way to the top. Your dreams could come true while in this job. There's no end to the heights you can climb. Now, come with me."

There was a gigantic hole in the middle of the capital. It was fifty meters across. Looking down from the ground level, it appeared pitch-black, ominous, and endless.

"…Are you sure this thing has a bottom?"

It was so eerie that people would've believed him if he said it was connected to hell or the realm of the dead. This was apparently the excavation point.

They descended into the endless pit using a lift connected by a flimsy cable. They went down—two hundred meters, then three hundred.

"These are the front lines that bolster the Empire's prosperity." In the quiet lift, only the site foreman's voice sounded out. "We call it the Planet's Navel. I'm not sure where that name came from, but you'll mine for the iron and rare metals that are crucial for maintaining the Empire's glory. The work seems simple enough, right?"

"...What happens once it's all gone?" Crossweil asked— foolishly. Though he had murmured it to himself, the foreman turned to him.

"Then we'd move on to a new energy source."

"...?"

They would simply find a new vein.

That was the answer Crossweil expected, but instead he received an indecipherable response to his inquiry. *A new energy source? What did that even mean?*

"Um!" The moment Crossweil attempted to ask another question, the lift clunked to a halt.

"Welcome to the world four thousand meters underground."

The lift's doors opened. Where the foreman pointed ahead was indeed the underground world.

The mines that opened out in front of them were surrounded by brown and gray bedrocks. Because the space was lit by the orange lights, it was bright as day, but if an accident severed any of the power supply cables, they would surely have been encapsulated by a darkness deeper than night.

"Let me show you the work you novices will be doing. Your job is to maintain the drills here."

They craned their necks to look up at the monolithic drill. The depths of the earth were mined not by human hands but by machines. In fact, all of the people employed here were primarily there to maintain the equipment.

"How do we do that?"

"Ask the other miners. I have a meeting with the capital officials right after this. I'm the project manager, after all."

Then he simply returned to the surface just like that. Left behind in the vein, the boys and girls, Crossweil included, looked at each other with dispirited expressions.

The excavation point four thousand meters underground.

They were C-class miners, and as apprentices, their job was to maintain the drills in the deepest mine of the Imperial capital.

"...They made it sound fancy like that, but really we're just doing menial labor."

There were mechanics there to repair the machinery.

Even if any of them had shown an interest in swapping out the drill bits that were used to crack through the hard rock, the miners wouldn't have been allowed to lay a finger on the machinery.

So, what was their job, then? It was simply to transport the machine parts.

"We just put the lubricants and new parts into containers and bring the broken ones up to the surface... I mean, calling it maintenance sounds a lot nicer."

In reality, it was just manual labor where they carried around parts that weighed dozens of kilograms. On top of that, it was boiling hot underground, and the air was thin.

"…So this is why…they have to…recruit people…"

The sweat was endless, too. Just making one round trip from one side of the mining area to the other was enough to sap him of his strength.

"It's hot and muggy… it reeks of oil, and to top it all off…they're breaking a lot of labor laws. No wonder they're losing workers."

He was getting front-row seats to where the labor shortage was coming from.

The young men and women coming to the capital for high-paying jobs were being driven to quit one after another by the intolerable work conditions.

"…I get it now. This is hell…I got myself a job in hell."

He took a short break. He didn't even have the strength to carry his own body weight and had collapsed directly onto the ground. Crossweil absentmindedly stared at the rock surrounding the mining site.

"Oh. Tuckered out already, Crow?"

Grinning, Eve was staring down at him. The shirt she wore looked like it'd seen better days.

"What do you think? Pretty bad line of work we've gotten ourselves into, right? Alice and I fell right over from the fatigue on our first day, too."

"Crow, are you doing okay?" Alicerose gave him a worried look. Though she also wore a shabby shirt like her twin, there was something alluring about the faint sheen of sweat coating her face.

"…The difference is ridiculous. It's like coming across an angel after seeing an imp from hell."

"Who's supposed to be the imp in this scenario?" Eve pinched his cheek.

The twins had been tasked with the job of carrying bottles of water and lunches to the miners. Though the work wasn't nearly as rigorous as transporting machine parts, it still took a toll on them.

"How many years have you worked here again?" Crossweil asked.

"Hm? What? You thinking of quitting already?" Eve sat down cross-legged on the spot. "Alice and I have been here for exactly a year. I think there were originally fifty recruits, but only seven or eight ended up sticking around for that whole time."

"...Are you supposed to be the cream of the crop or something?"

"If you stay on that long, you get a better assessment," Eve explained. "Plus, we're sending money home."

"And we get free lunch out of it," Alicerose added, letting out a small giggle. "Saving on lunch is a way bigger deal than you'd think. And you can use the facility showers, so you don't have to bathe at home."

"Oh, right. Alice is a regular at the showers." A bold smile spread across Eve's face. "She abused the facilities so much that they even reprimanded her."

"E-Eve?!"

"But the showers here are shared between men and women. The guys always make such a big deal out of it, too. They couldn't care less when I line up to rinse off, but when Alice does, they just let her take their spot in line. And she just thanks them and laughs about it. Must be nice, getting things only because of your looks."

"I-it's not like that at all!" Alicerose said. "Sh-she's completely twisting things, Crow!"

"Quit grumbling! I haven't twisted anything. I see you using your feminine wiles!"

"Eep?!" Eve made her way behind Alice and grabbed her twin's curvaceous rump this time.

Alice's scream echoed throughout the mines.

"S-stop, Eve...Crow can see!"

"You're the one who's always acting sexy, no matter the time or place!"

"Th-the people around us are staring, too!"

"Because you're always showing off! These humongous things! Oh, so *now* you're embarrassed?!"

The two were having a full-blown scuffle now. The younger one was blushing beet-red as she tried to flee from her older sister, who chased after her. Crossweil had gathered that this was an everyday occurrence.

"...I'm just going to keep taking my break over here," Crossweil said, still lying on the ground. He closed his eyes.

4

The deepest point of the Empire, the Planet's Navel.

Before he knew it, Crossweil had been working four thousand meters underground—a distance great enough to make him feel faint—for eleven whole days. As he'd gotten used to the work, everything around him had started to change, too.

He'd made friends with his coworkers.

"Morning, Crow! You look dead tired even though we're just getting started for today!"

"I've had my hands full since morning dealing with my sisters..."

A brown-haired girl named Musha sprinted past him. She rivaled Eve as the smallest girl in the mining shaft and was just fourteen. She also happened to be the youngest out of all of them. According to her, she'd come to work in the Empire and strike out on her own after having a fight with her parents.

She was cheerful and talked about her story like none of the events had happened to her, keeping a positive perspective.

But then Eve came by next.

"Watch it, Crow. She's nice to all the guys around here, regardless of who they are," Eve warned.

"Hunh? I'm kind to everyone, not just the guys," Musha shot back. "You're the only one I don't get along with, runt!"

"What?! You call *me* the runt?! You're way smaller than me!"

Crossweil watched the exchange, feeling entertained.

"Aren't they the best of friends?" Alicerose laughed under her breath. "All the kids working here are like that. It's easy to talk to everyone since we're all the same age, and we eat together, so it's almost like we're family. And that includes you now too, Crow."

"...Alice, you're not going to stop them?"

"Drake will stop them," Alicerose said, and almost as though she had timed it, a loud clap echoed through the place as someone clapped their hands together.

"Time for the morning meeting. I have a special announcement for you all today," said Drake, a brown-haired boy. He'd been working at the mines for three years. He was also their leader and was turning nineteen that year.

"You may see a guest in the afternoon. They will be observing the mines."

"A guest?" Eve opened her eyes wide and looked puzzled. "What are they coming for? Who are they?"

"A special observation team. All I've heard is that it's someone very high up in the Empire, so even Lavitch has been nervous since morning. I think they must be very important."

"Heh… The kind of person I hate the most, then."

"We received an order for this afternoon," Drake continued. "Once we're called, everyone present should stop working and gather here."

Then they split up. A dozen or so of the miners returned to their posts. Crossweil, of course, was tasked with the job of carrying parts back and forth.

"…"

He looked up at the staggering drill that was separated by an imposing barricade. He had started to get a full picture of the machine over the last two weeks he had been working as a miner. And so…

"There's definitely something off," he said to himself.

"Hey, Crow, what're you standing around doing nothing for?" Eve elbowed him from behind. "The leader's nice, but if that yappy foreman sees you, you'll be in for it. He's already on edge from the inspection in the afternoon."

"So, Eve, I was thinking…"

"Nobody wants to know what you think," she said. "But I guess I'll listen. What is it?"

"Is this *really* a mining facility?"

They were mining for iron ore. At least, that was the pretense for why they had gathered here, in the depths of the earth.

"I've never seen any ore being excavated. I asked Musha and Drake, and they haven't seen it, either. Plus, Drake's been here three years now."

"…"

"Has anyone seen the ore at all?" Crossweil continued.

They were in the deepest part of the Imperial capital, the Planet's Navel. Wasn't the whole point of that to mine for ore?

"I've been wondering if we've really been digging for something else," Crossweil said.

"Oh? Thinking like a little investigator, huh, Crow?" Eve gave a snort of laughter. "What good is it going wondering about such philosophical questions when we're just the underlings?"

"You've never been curious, Eve?"

"Not really. I don't care what we're mining for. It could be oil or dinosaur bones, for all I know. We just dig down. Then we earn money. That's all—" Eve cut herself off.

Just then, there was a commotion at the lift.

"Everyone gather round! Get into a line!" Lavitch's voice rang out through the mining site.

"Oh, crap…it's already time. This is such a chore," Eve said, clucking her tongue as she ran off. The miners lined up, surrounding the lift. Once Crossweil arrived, everyone had already taken their positions.

"Wait right here and clap when you see the Crown Prince!"

"…The Crown Prince?"

"No way! As in the Lord's son?"

Eve and Alicerose glanced at each other. Next to them, Musha and Drake looked bewildered, as they could have never imagined such an important guest would come.

Ting-a-ling.

A lift descended from above their heads.

"The Crown Prince has arrived!"

"His Highness, Yunmelngen, is here to conduct a personal inspection. Everyone, applaud now!"

First, the escorts disembarked. Ten very burly men, each

wearing suits, filed out. Behind them, the Crown Prince followed, his hair a bright blue and wearing a pristine white outfit.

"What the—?! Is he the real deal?!" Musha, who had shouted that out loud unintentionally, covered her mouth with her hands in a panic. It was unclear whether the Crown Prince had noticed.

"It's a pleasure to meet you," he said with a serene smile and clear voice.

He sounded like a boy soprano. There was an ambiguous note to his voice. It was almost as though it wasn't quite clear whether he was a girl or a boy who had yet to reach puberty.

The same went for his features. His eyes were wide as a kitten's, and his nose and lips were small. Though he had been presented as the Lord's one and only son, here in front of them all today, the Crown Prince seemed like a delicate and sweet girl.

"There really is something elegant about him."

"Hmph, I don't know about that," Eve huffed in response to Alicerose's murmur. "Why does he look so dainty. He's a guy. I can tell from his face he's never done a lick of work in his life."

"Do you think so?"

"Obviously," Eve said. "He's the Crown Prince. He's not elegant—what you're picking up on is the conceit written all over his face."

"He might be cuter than you, Eve," Alicerose commented.

"Really, Alice?"

Away from the two bickering twins, Crossweil was absent-mindedly staring at the Crown Prince's back as the foreman led him away.

…He's inspecting this place?

…A single bit of ore hasn't been dug up, though. What's he coming to look at, then?

There were plenty of mines and excavation sites all around the Empire. From among all of them, why had he chosen this place?

"..."

One hour passed.

Even after the Crown Prince had finished his inspection and left for the surface, that question remained in Crossweil's mind.

5

The Imperial streets were stained red.

It was twilight.

Crossweil and the other miners, grimy from a day's work, were just about to head home when Lavitch stopped them. It wasn't often that the foreman himself would call them back.

"Huh?! We're all getting special bonuses?!"

"That's right. It's a gift from Prince Yunmelngen. He wants you all to keep up the good work," Lavitch told them.

"Oh, we definitely will! Thank you, Mister Crown Prince, sir! Oh, I love him!" Eve clutched the envelope containing her bonus to her chest as she leapt with joy.

They had never been given such special treatment in the past.

"Ahh, the Crown Prince is so amazing," she said. "I could immediately see the elegance exuding from his face. I wonder if he might stop by again for another inspection tomorrow. Then maybe he could give us another bonus."

"You really are simple, Eve," Alicerose remarked, staring at her older sister.

"Say, Alice, what do you think of having a feast tonight?"

"What? We're not gonna save it, Eve?"

"Why would I do that, you dummy? It's my personal philosophy not to plan for tomorrow. Hey, Crow, you can head home early to put away the laundry. Alice and I are going grocery shopping!"

"Yeah, take your… Wait, they're already gone."

The two sisters had run off before he knew it. As instructed, he left straight for home.

He was walking toward the house, with his hand gripped tightly around the envelope holding his bonus, when…

"Hm?"

He heard someone running after him from behind. Were his sisters back? As he turned around, expecting to see them, his bonus was snatched right out of his hand.

"Wha?!"

He should have put the envelope in his pocket.

He didn't even have the time to react. The boy ran past Crossweil, envelope in hand. The crowd parted for the boy, and he was gone before Crossweil knew it.

"W-wait!"

The thief had been a small boy. Though his shirt and pants were plain, he had worn a distinct hat on his head. Its purpose was most likely to obscure the boy's face from Crossweil, but it was also perfect for tracking in the crowd.

"Hey! I'm going to get in trouble if you steal that!"

Though he was upset at losing his bonus, he was more frightened of his sisters' wrath.

He ran at full speed through the capital streets. The thief was obviously a minor. Crossweil knew he could beat the kid in both speed and stamina, but…that only applied in ideal circumstances.

47

Right now, after he had been toiling away and sweating up a storm all day, that wasn't the case. Exhausted, he couldn't run as fast as usual.

"Damn it. This just had to happen when I'm exhausted...!"

Though he wasn't able to close the distance between them, he wasn't letting the boy out of his sight. They kept up their race, and the thief was the first to give up. He turned a corner and headed down a back alley.

"Uh? This kid..."

The thief couldn't have been a local. Up ahead was a dead end. Even Crossweil knew that, so the rest of the Imperial capital residents would have, too.

"Huh!"

Just as Crossweil expected, the boy in the hat stopped in his tracks. Walls surrounded him on all three sides. He had nowhere to go.

"I've got you now, you idiot!"

"Whoa, we've lost. You won by a landslide! We give up!"

"What are you talking about? There's no 'we' in this. The only royal 'we' here is a royally-screwed thief."

He pinned the boy's arms from behind.

...?

...*What is with this kid?*

He'd been able to tell that the boy was tiny, but when he actually held on to him, Crossweil thought he was even scrawnier and more powerless than he imagined.

"U-unhand us! Stop! If you're too rough, our hat will—ah!"

The boy squirmed in Crossweil's grip. In his struggle, the hat the boy was wearing low on his face flew off.

...Which revealed his strikingly blue hair as it settled softly into place. Then Crossweil saw the boy's delicate features as well. As he stared at the thief's profile, illuminated by the evening sun...

"Huh! It's you!"

"...Ah-ha-ha. You got us there."

It was the Crown Prince, Yunmelngen. The Crown Prince whose eyes he had met briefly at the inspection was here, in front of his eyes, smiling sheepishly.

Crossweil was, of course, bewildered.

...*Wait a second.*

...*What is he doing here? Why's he stealing stuff? What's happening?*

The kid gave Crossweil a knowing look.

"Y-you do know who we are, don't you? Let us go."

"..." Crossweil silently thought for a while. Ultimately, he decided to pretend he didn't recognize the prince. "I bet you're just a doppelgänger."

"What?!"

"I have no idea who you are, and I don't remember seeing you anywhere. You're a thief who stole my money. I'm taking you straight to the police."

"Huh?!"

The color drained from the prince look-alike's face.

"J-just wait! Y-you can't. That would create an uproar!"

"You already made a spectacle of things yourself, I'd say," Crossweil replied.

"We didn't mean anything bad by it!"

"Sure seems like something a criminal would say. Uh, if I remember correctly, the closest police station would be..."

"W-wait! All right...then let's make a deal. We will give you ten times the amount of this bonus. So please, let this be the end of it."

"Oh, where could a police officer be…"

"Listen to us!"

The culprit started to thrash about. Since he was so scrawny and small, he couldn't escape from Crossweil's grip no matter how hard he tried.

"You want to pay me ten times this? Then why'd you go to all the trouble stealing it in the first place?"

"It's true! Who do you think we are?!"

"I have no idea," Crossweil shot back.

"Look! Look at our face!"

Since the kid was just asking him to look, he did turn to face the boy, staring at his profile from up close.

Eve had described his face as "dainty," and it did have a sort of charm to it, with its long eyelashes and the large, adorable catlike pupils. He didn't look quite like a boy or a girl—he was androgynous.

"The Crown Prince Yunmelngen."

"Yes!"

"…Almost looks like you, you fake. Let's add fraud to your list of crimes, then."

"No! No!" The kid started to struggle again. "Don't you see the elegance in our face, in our voice?! It's practically oozing from our whole body!"

"Doesn't seem very 'elegant' to describe yourself like that."

"…We are warning you. Roughhouse us anymore, and we'll tell the guards about it. Is that what you want?"

"…?" Crossweil couldn't understand what the thief was getting at. Even if, in the slightest chance this kid were important, the Crown Prince was just a title given to the successor to the throne in this country.

"You are so discourteous," the boy continued.

Even when pinned in Crossweil's grip, the boy seemed to be looking down on him.

"You've manhandled us and haven't even noticed?"

"..."

That didn't seem like something a boy would say, but at the same time, Crossweil didn't feel like he was touching a girl, either. He didn't know what to believe.

"......Well, it's fine. I'm starting to get tired anyway," Crossweil said.

He let the boy loose. They were at a dead end, anyway. The kid had nowhere to run, even if he wasn't holding on to him.

"C'mon, cough it up."

"Well, if we must," the boy said. "But you would do well to make sure it's not stolen again."

"You sure are condescending for being the thief who took it."

"We are not a thief. We are the Crown Prince."

The would-be Crown Prince obediently handed back the envelope. Then he picked up the hat on the ground, dusted it off with his hands, and continued, "We have no interest in physical attachments. We were simply curious as to what would happen if we stole it."

"Well, obviously you would've been caught by me," Crossweil replied.

"We wanted to know how the people would react to having something they carry stolen so suddenly. Whether they would shout or create a scene. Also...how they would behave upon realizing who we are. We thought you would be shocked and apologetic."

"...Hunh?"

"We have no earthly desires," the Crown Prince Yunmelngen said, holding his hat to his chest. "This hat, these clothes, we can obtain anything we want. But because we lack worldly desires, we instead have an interest in obtaining knowledge."

"...So what? You just spend all your time satisfying your intellectual curiosity or something?"

That seemed very much like a philosophical problem only the Crown Prince would have. If the kid had been facing Eve, she definitely wouldn't have hesitated to drop-kick him for even uttering that sentence out loud.

...He seems like the real deal.

...His explanation for stealing from me is too weird to make up.

It seemed he actually wasn't an imposter, then. This was in fact Crown Prince Yunmelngen, who had come to observe them that very afternoon.

"No, wait. I don't care who you are. You still stole my cash."

"Please, just pretend it never happened." The kid stared at him like a kitten begging for food. "Yes, we know just the thing!"

The Crown Prince clapped his hands, as though he'd realized something.

"If you'll see it in your heart to let bygones be bygones, then we will give you a special honor!"

"What honor?"

"You will be given the privilege of being our conversation partner!" The Crown Prince flung open his arms. "We were just looking for someone to fill the role. Father is always so busy. And we are so bored but want to know more about the people."

"Wait. That doesn't benefit me at all."

"You would be our conversation partner," the Crown Prince said. "That should make you happier than any other person in the world, shouldn't it?"

"..."

There was a sparkle in the boy's eyes. But Crossweil coldly stared down at him.

"All right." Crossweil grabbed the prince's wrist. "I think I *will* turn you in to the police."

"Why would you do that?!"

And so, Crossweil's life in the capital began, living with the Nebulis twins and now spending his days with an eccentric.

MEMORY ILLUMINATION 2

The Day the Planet Wept

1

It had been five weeks since Crossweil had come to the capital.

His everyday life had been entirely changed.

He spent six days a week at his job. And the remaining day would be spent cleaning and doing the laundry all morning. Then he would meal prep for the rest of the week and package everything away to store it.

Once he'd finished all of that...

"Heeey, Crow? Where do you think you're going?"

"...On a walk," he answered Eve casually.

Then Crossweil left home.

He headed to an alley off of Eleventh Avenue. It was the exact spot he'd first talked to the so-called thief. He arrived at the usual empty lot nearby.

Once he had reached his destination, he heard the endearing mewl of a cat.

"Ah-ha-ha, looks like you guys aren't doing too shabby."

The Crown Prince Yunmelngen was there, feeding the stray cats. He wore the same plain clothes when Crossweil had first met him, along with the hat meant to cover his face.

"Oh, it's you, Crow!" Yunmelngen seemed thrilled to see Crossweil as he pulled off his cap.

"I can barely tell which one of you's the cat," Crossweil commented.

"Hm? What's that supposed to mean?" The Crown Prince gave Crossweil a reproachful look. But the boy didn't seem altogether displeased, and his tone was upbeat. "Well, it's fine. Come, over here," the prince said, using some leftover iron poles in place of a chair.

Yunmelngen pointed next to him and motioned for Crossweil to join him.

He was the Crown Prince's conversation partner.

Meeting here had become just another part to his routine, and something he'd done three times already. Yunmelngen was generally the one doing the talking while he listened. During the few times Yunmelngen would tire himself out, Crossweil would make small talk.

"We were very interested in what the public bathhouses are like," the prince said. "A gigantic private bath is always prepared for us to bathe in, after all."

"You say it like it's obvious, but I have no idea how you wash up."

"We have just told you, then," Yunmelngen said matter-of-factly.

"We wanted to see what the women's baths were like. And what would happen if we entered one?" The Crown Prince continued.

"......Come again?"

"But when we did that, we were caught and there was such a scene."

Hee-hee, the prince laughed as he teasingly stuck out his tongue.

"Ahh, it was such an ordeal. Even worse than when we stole your bonus, Crow. We had to work so hard to hush it up so it wouldn't make the papers."

"…What kind of perverted guy are you?"

"Hm? Did we ever say we were a 'guy'?"

From the side, Crossweil saw the corners of Yunmelngen's lips rise mischievously. He was reminded again of how androgynous the kid appeared.

"Actually, there was a commotion when we peeked into the men's bath too," the prince continued.

"So you're a repeat offender!"

"No, no, first we peeked into the men's bath, then the women's. We just wanted to see what would happen with both of them, since we can pass as either gender. So we just wanted to do an experiment."

"…You're just creating problems for others, then."

"But it was so delightful."

Yunmelngen laughed again.

It seemed the Crown Prince had a habit of wreaking chaos all over the capital. Making those issues go away was likely a tall order for the vassals.

"That was all we wanted to talk about." Yunmelngen stood up.

He brushed off the dirt from his bottom and pulled the hat he held low over his face. It seemed that was all for their conversation that day.

The Crown Prince had very little free time. And with how long it took to make a round trip from the Castle Tower Seat, it meant they had twenty minutes to talk at most.

"We will be taking our leave," Yunmelngen said.

"Right," Crossweil replied.

"So, the next opening in our schedule is…nine days from now at four in the afternoon. Well, there you have it!"

"Huh?! Aren't you going to ask me if I've got plans?! I have a job!"

"We will be waiting here."

The eccentric prince waved as he blended into the crowd on Eleventh Avenue.

2

Nine days later.

Crossweil glanced at the clock on the wall of his home.

"…Why am I even keeping an eye on the time?" he commented.

The rendezvous had been thrust upon him without his consent. He had work that day, of course…or rather, he should have been at work. They'd ended up leaving in the afternoon. The Imperial higher-ups wanted another inspection, and so, he and the rest of the miners had been shooed away from the site.

"Can't help but think it's the Crown Prince doing something behind the scenes…"

It was three in the afternoon. He'd gone every time he'd been called by the prince, but he had a growing suspicion their relationship was warping into one of servitude. That was when he'd started to get cold feet.

"…Tsk. Fine. If he just wants to meet, then I'll at least do that."

He stood up, his body leaden. He decided to buy a snack on the way from one of the stalls. Crossweil wondered how the prince would think of a commoner's snack.

"Hey, Crow." As he was thinking that, Eve returned home. "Could you repair the roof?"

"What?"

"According to the weather report, there's supposed to be a big storm tonight. That spot you fixed up earlier came loose, and we've got a draft coming in."

Wait, he almost said out loud, barely stopping himself. The timing was just awful.

"Um, but I have plans right now..."

"Your priority should be fixing up that roof."

"..."

He couldn't say anything.

She was right. He knew about the storm forecast, too. The patch coming off and resulting draft were both his mistakes, after all.

But he had plans...

"We're counting on you. Alice and I are going to shop for tonight's dinner."

"......Got it," he said. His voice was weak, but that was all he could say.

Just like his sister had said, the roof was leaky. He finished in half the time, likely because he had experience now.

However...

It was five.

By the time he put away the tools, it was too late.

"..."

The sky above was full of bulky, gloomy rain clouds.

He couldn't tell when it would start pouring. Even the passersby on the main road were walking quickly, as though they were wary of the rain.

"I never managed to make it..."

It was an hour after the meeting time. He'd stood up the

Crown Prince. The prince also was so busy he only had the chance to sneak out of his residence after a nine-day wait. There was no way he would have been able to stay more than an hour for the meeting. He probably wasn't there at the empty lot anymore.

As a commoner who stood up the prince, after they had already waited days for their schedule to open up, Crossweil had likely used up all the Yunmelngen's goodwill.

Yes. It was the prince's first outing in nine days.

"Uh…wait."

But then he realized there was another way of thinking about it. Until then, he had only been seeing it from his own perspective, so it hadn't fully occurred to him.

…*He decided on the time without even asking me.*

…*And I've even complained about how he never takes my schedule into account.*

In that case, had Crossweil ever thought about the Crown Prince's schedule?

"He made time in his busy schedule…and he chose to spend that time with me."

The prince's limited free time was more valuable than even an entire fortune. Considering that, how could he just write the prince off and assume Yunmelngen had gone straight home?

Crossweil had no idea if Yunmelngen had already left.

"Uh!"

Before he even realized what he was doing, Crossweil had practically kicked down the front door and sprinted outside.

He ran as fast as he could down the main street. He ran past the workers and families on their way home, toward the Eleventh Avenue dead end, and was out of breath.

"Haah…ugh…haah…uh……"

It was half past five now.

He arrived at the dead end's small clearing just as it was growing dark.

There crouched Yunmelngen, unmoving and surrounded by kittens.

"..."

Crossweil had no idea whether it was his ragged breathing or footsteps that gave him away, but the moment Yunmelngen noticed he was there; the prince raised his face.

Crossweil couldn't tell if the prince was angry or forlorn. His eyes were filled with an eddy of emotions that never quite tipped to one side or the other.

"Um..."

As those giant eyes stared straight at Crossweil, he could only scratch the back of his head.

"...Sorry. I ran a little late."

He didn't bother mentioning the roof he had repaired. The excuse would have meant nothing to the prince, after all.

"This is a first for us," Yunmelngen murmured in a small voice. He sighed. "This is the first time in our life this has happened, that anyone has reneged on a promise and made us wait for eternity."

"..."

"I see. So this empty feeling is what it feels like to have a promise broken. We have learned something new today...and that some things are better left never learned at all. We will consider this new insight to be enough for this meeting."

The Crown Prince looked up at the rain clouds. Droplets were falling down onto his blue bangs.

"It's raining. Did you finish repairing the roof in time?"

"......Huh?!"

"Well, of course we would look into who you are and where you live. We would never simply meet with a person we didn't know." Finally, finally, Yunmelngen's lips formed a slight smile. "But we must go home now. We are quite busy and have yet another meeting to attend this evening."

"...I'm sorry."

"Really now." The prince sighed.

He had produced a comm contained in a tasteful small box.

"We had someone buy this for us. It's the LinLin-X6, the newest model available. If you plan on being late, you ought to send an apology."

The prince thrust it at him.

"...This is for me?"

"Make sure to keep it with you always," Yunmelngen continued. "We have also inputted our private address in the contacts."

Crossweil hadn't been expecting this at all. He had thought the prince would cast him aside, but instead he made it easier to meet each other.

"Also, as you know, we are the Crown Prince, so the vassals will become suspicious if you call us too often."

"...I wouldn't just ring you up," Crossweil said.

"You must answer within five seconds of our call," Yunmelngen added.

"Now that's unreasonable!"

"And you may not include any other addresses in the contacts."

"Those are some unreasonable demands! ...Then again, I don't have anyone else I'd call regularly."

His sisters wouldn't have an expensive comm like this. Neither would his friends at the excavation site.

"Then until next time," Yunmelngen said. "Two in the afternoon, eight days from now!"

As the rain began to pour down, Yunmelngen ran toward the main street with only his hat to protect him from the rain.

Crossweil saw the eccentric prince off, then headed home in the pelting rain.

"I'm home," he said.

"What the heck, Crow! Where did you go in the middle of this downpour?!"

"Why, you're soaking wet, Crow!" Alice shouted.

The sisters rushed to his side as soon as he entered.

"What's gotten into you?! We need to get you changed before you catch a cold!"

"I-it's okay, I'm fine," he said as Alicerose handed him a towel. On the other hand, Eve let out a lofty chuckle and her eyes had an odd glint to them.

"I know what happened, Alice!" she declared. "It must be a girl! He's just come back from a secret lovers' tryst!"

"Crow was with a girl?! So you were out on a date, then?!"

"No!"

He'd just been talking. There hadn't been any dating involved. He also wasn't even certain whether the person he was meeting was male or female.

"I see. Uh-huh. So you've got a girlfriend. Hee-hee. You've grown up, Crow," Alicerose said. "Agh! I think I feel more embarrassed than you do about it!"

"...Wait, why are you blushing?" Crossweil asked. "And also, I don't have a girlfriend to begin with."

"You'd better introduce her, Crow. And tell us who she is!"

"Like I said, there's no one!"

That night, Crossweil was further interrogated by his bright-eyed sisters about the person he was meeting.

3

Eight days later, two in the afternoon.

He was at the usual clearing by the dead end at the time Yunmelngen had indicated.

"…He's so late."

However, Yunmelngen never came. Realizing he couldn't be late again, Crossweil had come thirty minutes early and had even wondered whether he had gotten the time right as he nervously waited. But the meeting time had long passed.

"Is this payback for last time?" he asked out loud. "Seriously…"

The comm rang. A light melody came from the device.

"Hey there."

It was Yunmelngen's voice.

His usual levity was missing, however. In fact, it seemed weak and more of a hoarse whisper than anything.

"You sound like it's the end of the world or something," Crossweil remarked.

"We caught a cold…this sore throat has ruined our voice."

The prince cleared his throat.

"It seems we caught one from being in the rain while waiting for a certain someone."

"…"

Right…

As soon as the prince mentioned a cold, Crossweil pieced the puzzle together.

"I'm sorry about earlier. So, what would you like to do? Do you want me to buy something and bring it to you?"

"Yes, thank you."

"Hey! Wait, that was a joke!"

"We will invite you to the Castle Tower Seat as a guest."

"I said wait!"

The Castle Tower Seat was, of course, the residence of the Lord himself. And he, a mere commoner, was supposed to enter that domain? He was also wearing a plain shirt that day. He would surely be stopped at the gate by the guards, and that would be that.

"We will send you information for a secret route right now."

The comm rang again. A map with the Lord's residence at its center appeared on the screen. It was even marked with a blue line that led him from his current location to the building.

"......Hm? But this doesn't lead to the Castle Tower Seat?" Crossweil asked.

Instead, it led to the low hills right behind the residence.

"This is how we normally return."

"But aren't you there right now?"

"It is a secret path. Haven't you learned about it in history class? Every head of state prepares an emergency escape route in every era, just in case the unthinkable happens."

"I know that much."

"The hills have a hidden passage that connects to the Castle Tower Seat."

"Wait. That sounds like something you definitely shouldn't be telling me!"

There was no question this was a national secret. If anyone found out that the Crown Prince had leaked the Lord's residence's secret escape route, it would be a scandal. And he would be in danger for even knowing about it.

"We are just a child. If we let a secret slip, who's to chide us, considering we're a minor."

"…That's no excuse."

"But do be careful. We'll have a huge problem on our hands if you get caught."

"I genuinely hope that this secret route thing isn't real," Crossweil answered with reluctance and started walking toward his destination.

It took him about thirty minutes.

"…It was seriously real?" Crossweil said in a stupor.

The hill looked down upon the capital and overlooked the reddish-brown Castle Tower Seat.

There was a hidden passageway.

He was in the woods about fifty meters behind the stone monument that commemorated the hill.

When he thrust his hand between a giant pile of boulders, his fingertips were met with a switch, cool to the touch. The moment he pressed it, the space between the boulders opened up several centimeters and created a hole just large enough for a single person to pass through.

"Is the coast clear?"

"Yeah, there were some people on top of the hill, but nobody was wandering toward the woods."

"Then enter. Once you're inside, flip the switch and the door will close."

"…Okay."

One mystery down.

He'd wondered how Yunmelngen was frequently able to slip

away from home. It seemed the prince had been giving his guards the slip by using the secret route.

"I'm still not so sure you should have told me about this, though..."

The passage descended underground. It had likely been made decades ago. The path was narrow and filled with the smell of dust and mildew.

He headed down the hill toward the area beneath the Lord's residence. From there, he headed up a set of spiral stairs and hesitantly opened the door to the emergency exit.

It led to a dazzling inner palace decorated with stained glass.

"What the... Am I really inside Castle Tower Seat?"

He hadn't been caught by the guards or seen on any security cameras. A regular commoner like himself had snuck right in. It would be a catastrophe if any unsavory characters discovered the route.

"Hope I never sleep talk or anything..."

A gigantic door decorated in a gold design towered in front of him.

"Are you here?"

"I'm on the fifth floor of this super-decked-out building and in front of a super-fancy door," Crossweil answered. "I'm kind of worried that guards might storm in at any second."

"Then I'm going to open it. Come inside once it is."

Creak...

The mechanical door opened with an imposing sound.

A lit chandelier hung from the ceiling and an expensive-looking custom carpet was at his feet. Paintings reminiscent of the ages lined the walls. Even the view made him feel as if he was in the penthouse of a suite in a hotel.

"I feel like your furniture's worth a thousand or ten thousand times more than ours…"

"Admire the furniture all you want, but isn't it customary to start with a greeting for the person you're visiting?"

The canopied bed was surrounded by a pearly lace curtain. Yunmelngen weakly motioned for him to approach while still lying down.

"…Hello," the prince said.

"You don't look like you're doing so hot. Oh, I bought this in town. It's pudding. Have some."

"That's pretty thoughtful of you, Crow. We are not sure whether we will enjoy it, but that aside…ack…" The prince coughed right as he smiled.

"Are you really sure you're okay?"

"We are much better compared to before, though it may not seem that way. Our body was never particularly hardy. We are as sickly and ephemeral as a flower…ahh, we hope to say goodbye to this way of life soon."

"Hm?"

Something felt off. What did the prince mean about saying goodbye to life?

"Soon, the world as we know it will be transformed." As Yunmelngen lay recumbent, he looked up at the canopy of the bed.

"Humans will soon obtain a new form of energy," he continued. "There is even a chance that it will heal our frail constitution. I'm sure you must be looking forward to it, too, Crow."

"…"

What was the prince talking about?

He had known Yunmelngen was eccentric since they day they'd met, but this was the first time he hadn't been able to follow the prince's words in the slightest.

"Sorry, but I'm not sure what you mean," Crossweil said.

"You're all excavating it, aren't you? The energy that lies at the deepest point in the planet may bring us miracles yet."

He was digging for that?

...An energy sleeping at the deepest point in the planet? What's that even supposed to mean?

...We're just mining metal veins. Just iron ore and rare metals. However...

The excavation site was called the Planet's Navel, and not a single soul had seen iron ore being extracted from the place.

"I think we're talking about entirely different things here. We've just been mining for iron ore over at the site."

"What?"

"At least, that's what they've told the bottom rung."

"...Really?"

Now Yunmelngen went silent. He continued to look up as though he were earnestly thinking something over.

"Oh, we see. Then the information is being withheld from the citizens right now," the prince concluded.

"This is starting to sound dangerous..."

"Though we think they could just announce it. Are you curious? We are sure you must be."

To be frank, Crossweil didn't actually want to know.

Based on how Yunmelngen had just admitted the information was under a gag order, he wasn't foolish enough to not realize how dangerous it would be for a commoner like him to know the truth.

Despite understanding that, curiosity had gotten the better of him.

"...So the excavation isn't for ore, then?" Crossweil asked.

"That's right. Why, of course it wouldn't be. We would not have personally went to observe one of the many, many iron mines."

"…Right."

"We'll let you in on what's really going on as a special treat." Yunmelngen smiled. "You are digging up an entirely new energy source over there."

"What?"

"Humans live on but the surface of the planet. However, that energy flows within the deepest part of the planet, almost like lava. Periodically, this energy flows to an area very close to the surface. And, with a great amount of digging, one can make a fountain of it spout out of the planet."

"…A fountain from digging deep into the planet, huh?"

"So there you have it. "

"Right."

So that was the Planet's Navel.

They had created an excavation point in the center of the capital and had drilled down four thousand meters all to retrieve that energy.

"Why haven't they told the public about this?" Crossweil asked.

"We wouldn't know. It is one of the Lord and the Eight Great Elders' most secret projects, so perhaps they hope to make a great announcement to surprise the whole world over once the discovery is made."

It almost sounded too good to be true. Had Crossweil heard a story about some unfathomable energy sleeping in the depths of the planet on the streets of the Empire, he wouldn't have believed it.

"Doesn't it sound like a dream come true?" Yunmelngen smiled. "If they are able to excavate that energy, the whole world would be pushed forward an entire step into the future. There is even a possibility that medical technology could be developed so that colds like this can be cured instantly."

"Do you really think things would go that conveniently?"

"We are each free to dream," the prince answered, almost as though saying it to himself. He nodded, though weakly because of his sickness.

"And that day will be coming soon," he added.

"...When? When's this too-good-to-be-true future coming?"

"In about two weeks."

"That's a hundred times sooner than I imagined!"

"If not, we would never have inspected the place."

The prince was convincing. He had likely only paid a visit because the project was as good as complete.

"At the moment, you have reached a depth of four thousand eight hundred meters, yes? That yet-unknown energy has pooled five thousand meters below the planet's surface. You have just two hundred more to go."

"...It's practically right in front of us, then."

"As we said, the day our dreams become reality is near—"

Klack.

Right at that moment, they were both surprised by a rapping at the door.

"Oh no!" the prince cried. "It may be the physician or a vassal here to visit!"

Yunmelngen scowled.

"Hide, Crow!"

"Wh-where?!"

"Uh, behind the curtains... No, those are transparent, and the closet would not work...so under the bed!"

He dove under just as he was told. It was pitch-black, and all he could do was listen to know what was happening. He heard the door open.

"Crown Prince, Your Highness, how do you feel?"

"His Excellency the Lord is terribly worried."

"Please do take care of yourself. We have brought you gifts for our visit."

He heard their footsteps.

It sounded like it was three, or possibly four, people. No, there seemed to be many more. Seven...no, eight.

"...It's just a cold," the prince said. "You needn't come all the way here, Eight Great Elders. The vassals will believe we are frightfully ill."

The bed shook slightly.

Yunmelngen had likely sat up with as much enthusiasm as he could from the bed. He sounded more animated than he had just earlier, almost as though he hadn't been feeling unwell at all.

...Yunmelngen?

...You sound quite harsh right now.

But what he felt more unsettled by was the displeasure in Yunmelngen's voice.

"We will be back to official business tomorrow," the prince said. "See, we are quite fine."

"How terribly rude of us. We heard that Your Highness had run a high fever and was quite ill. Why, His Excellency even posed delaying the upcoming Festival of Spiritualism in two weeks' time."

"There is no need," the prince said in a sullen tone. "Now, you may take your leave. We are quite busy."

"As you wish. Please take care of yourself."

The eight sets of footsteps filed out of the room. The door shut on them, almost as though it were shooing them out.

"Ack...cough! ...Cough......ugh...ah...!" Yunmelngen fell to his knees.

He knelt on the carpeted floor, coughing terribly. Even from the bed, Crossweil could tell the state the boy was in.

"Yunmeln—"

"Wait!"

Crossweil attempted to crawl out from under the bed, but he was stopped by the prince.

"Wait. Wait until we say that you may leave..."

"...?"

"......We do not want you to see our nightclothes...as......well, then you would know..."

"Know? Know what?"

"...Please, just wait."

Yunmelngen almost collapsed back onto the bed. He struggled to breathe for some time after that.

"...Thank you for waiting."

Crossweil crawled out from under the bed. When Crossweil turned around, he found Yunmelngen flushed and covered by a blanket brought right up to his neck. The prince was staring back at him.

"...We would like you to be here, close to us, for longer."

"Like I said, what was that?"

"..." Yunmelngen looked up at the canopy. "Let us speak of hypotheticals. Suppose there are fathers who wish for daughters, and others who wish for sons."

"Well, obviously there are," Crossweil said.

"Just listen. We speak of a specific case. A father who lost his son too soon. And one who felt the need to protect his next son."

The whole conversation was so odd that Crossweil wasn't following. He had no idea what the Crown Prince was trying to tell him.

"So. Any child would be sensitive to a parent's affection, isn't that right? A child would know that, yes, their father wanted a son. And the child may try to fulfill their parent's wishes out of the desire for praise. In fact, one might try to lead a life to meet their parent's ideal expectations."

"…? I'm not following what you're saying here."

"The Festival of Spiritualism is coming up," the prince said.

"…And this is related to what you were saying how?"

"We simply returned to the subject at hand. We were just talking about it before the Eight Great Elders disturbed us."

An inexplicable energy that slumbered deep within the planet. And the Planet's Navel was the site of the energy's extraction.

"The Festival of Spiritualism commemorates reaching the deepest point of the excavation. As we said before, the deepest point, five thousand meters below, is just ahead of us."

"None of the miners have heard of this," Crossweil countered.

"The foreman likely is aware. We and the Lord will also attend the Festival of Spiritualism."

"The Lord?! …Oh, right," Crossweil remembered. "He's your dad."

Over time, he'd grown less sensitive to that feeling. They were having an ordinary conversation, but the person in front of him was indeed the Crown Prince.

…I was so surprised hearing the Lord would be making an appearance at the site, though.

…But it's already a big deal that the Crown Prince came for an inspection.

Just two hundred meters away.

A new type of energy slumbered down below where they dug, an unimaginable form of energy.

"There may be an announcement that the Planet's Navel is actually being used to excavate it. The Festival of Spiritualism's schedule has been finalized, after all."

"…This is all such a big deal it doesn't even feel real."

The whole world would likely be clamoring about it. Even Yunmelngen himself dreamed that this new energy would revolutionize the world.

"Well, all right. This isn't something commoners like me are supposed to even think about... Anyway, do you not like those eight vassal guys or whoever they were? You really sounded short with them."

"You mean the Eight Great Elders?"

The Lord's council was also known as the eight sages. They were each leaders in their fields—in medicine, chemistry, biology, physics, military studies, and linguistics.

"We don't fancy them," Yunmelngen answered. As he looked up, his eyes narrowed, and the disgust was obvious on his face. "The Lord has had ears only for them since their arrival. They've made him their puppet. Once we become Lord, we will be sure to drive them out."

"...Sounds like a lot of trouble, being the Crown Prince."

"But we're in a good mood today. Since you came, Crow— cough, ugh...cough...!" Yunmelngen doubled over. It seemed the prince was far from well.

"Don't strain yourself," Crossweil warned. "I should get going soon, too. Can I use the same route to get back?"

"...Cough...you may..."

"Make sure you rest up. You're going to at that Festival of Spiritualism event or whatever, right?"

"...Yes."

The prince seemed more docile than usual for whatever reason. He nodded weakly from his sickbed.

"...You may use the secret route you learned of whenever you would like, Crow."

4

Seven days later.

The deepest excavation point in the capital, the Planet's Navel, was suddenly all over the news.

"This is a big deal! Super big!"

They were four thousand eight hundred meters below the surface. The youngest girl, Musha, was running around, her expression entirely different from usual.

"Everyone, listen! Apparently we weren't mining for iron this whole time! Look at this article!"

A new resource mankind would obtain.

One that is neither gas, nor coal, nor petroleum. The Empire had reported this to the rest of the world: a magma-like new energy that flows beneath the planet's crust had been observed.

"...Seriously?"

Eve was aflutter, of course.

The excavation that had continued for an entire year was likely to go down in mankind's history as a great feat. And she probably felt proud knowing that.

"Say, Alice," she said. "Discovering a new energy source is a big deal, right? It is, right?"

"...Oh, y-yes. The TV did say that. You watched it too, Eve." Alicerose still seemed unsure of the news. "Maybe we'll all suddenly become famous?"

"And then what?"

"TV programs and news writers would call us. We'd go on TV and talk about how much we struggled up to now and how it was like to get the job done. Maybe we'll be able to have autobiographies that will be turned into movies."

"And then what?"

"We'd never have money troubles ever again, Eve!"

"That sounds amazing, Alicerose!"

""Yay!"" the two sisters squealed as they hugged.

The other workers were also trying to imagine their futures and were so restless they were hardly getting any work done.

"Is everyone here?" Their leader, Drake, had come down in the lift. "I have great news. It seems that His Excellency is giving every miner working here a bonus as soon as we reach the five-thousand-meter mark."

"No way!"

"I couldn't be happier!"

The entire excavation site was excited.

Giving his coworkers a sidelong glance, Crossweil snuck behind the lift. His comm in his breast pocket had been blinking since just earlier.

"How is it on-site?"

"I'm sure you can hear the excitement," he answered. "Everybody's enthusiastic. Especially with a bonus to look forward to."

"Ah-ha-ha. It's so easy to find a way into the hearts of the citizens."

He could hear Yunmelngen laugh on the other end. According to the prince, he had finally recovered in the last few days. His physicians had forbidden him from excursions, however.

"You should be grateful to us. We proposed the bonus to the Lord. We told him it was only proper to give the miners extra with the incoming astral power and Festival of Spiritualism."

"…Astral power?"

"That is the temporary name of the energy you are digging up. The Eight Great Elders took it from pictographs on some very old ruins. The name is quite poetic, wouldn't you say?"

77

"Well, that's neither here nor there, as far as I'm concerned."

"So, also, Crow…" He caught a sudden burst of playfulness in Yunmelngen's tone. **"Are you sad you haven't seen us?"**

"What?"

"We're sorry. Our physician still forbids us from any excursions, and we have our position as Crown Prince to think of, as well as preparations that must be made for the Astral Power Festival of Spiritualism. We understand how you feel, crying night after night as you are unable to reunite with us. Shall we send a personal picture for you to keep?"

"I'm hanging up now."

"Ahhh! Wait a moment! …You're no fun, Crow." The Crown Prince sighed. **"…The Lord and security will be present at the festival. We likely won't be able to speak at the event."**

"Then we can meet after."

"Yes! Now you've got it. That is what we wanted to say as well!"

Crossweil wished the prince had just come out and said it then, but before Crossweil could tell the prince that, Yunmelngen was already moving on.

"Then we shall convene the day after the festival. Three in the afternoon at the clearing!"

"What about *my* plans—"

"We will be waiting! We have another meeting with the Eight Great Elders! See you later!"

"…Geez, I can never get a word in edgewise."

The prince had already hung up. Crossweil was used to this, of course, seeing as how it happened all the time.

"…The day after the festival. Basically he's saying to keep my schedule clear."

From four thousand meters below the surface, Crossweil looked up toward the direction of the Crown Prince.

However...

Neither of them knew that their meeting would never come to be.

And of course, Crossweil nor the Crown Prince had any way of knowing that had been their final conversation as humans. The Imperial capital's collapse was approaching...

───────────────

"In seven more days."

The small room was dim—very dim.

A secret underground audience chamber below the Imperial assembly.

Upon closing the door, the secret room was fully isolated from the outside world. Not a single sound could escape. Even the Lord could not intercept the clandestine meetings that occurred in this room.

And there, in that very space...

The eight men and women known as the sages of the Empire sat facing one another.

"The inexplicable energy, the energy that the Astrals called astral power, has made an appearance."

"The enormous power that flows within the core of the planet. In the last century, no one has seen it rising to the surface."

"A vortex."

"It is overpowering. It will burst forth with a force even greater than a volcanic eruption. If the eruption were more powerful than we project it to be, it would easily cross the predicted explosion threshold."

Yes.

All of it would be a misfortunate accident—fully unintentional. The new energy five thousand meters below the surface would be too powerful and would blow away the entire excavation site along with the people surrounding it. And it would be no one's fault. In fact, no one would be able to prove that anyone had planned it at all.

"The Lord, Crown Prince, and other important persons watching the Festival of Spiritualism."

"Not a single one of them will survive."

Both the Lord and his successor would disappear. Once the supreme authority figures of the Empire were gone, the nation would likely be greatly shaken.

"Only the Eight Great Elders shall remain."

5

Morning, nine o'clock.

The peal of a trumpet resounded on Eleventh Avenue of the Imperial capital as the sky was dotted with multicolored balloons and flying confetti.

"Eve, Alice," Crossweil said, "we really need to get going or we'll be late."

"W-wait a second, Crow! ...Does my scarf look good wrapped this way? What do you think?"

"It takes time for a gal to get dolled up!"

He never would have imagined this day would come. His adoptive sisters were talking about "scarves" and getting "dolled up."

"I'll just wait outside," he told them.

He headed out of the junk house and squinted from the unusually bright sunlight. The weather was perfect for a ceremony.

"...Time just flew by," he commented.

They had finished their work in the Planet's Navel the night before.

At a total depth of four thousand nine hundred ninety-nine meters.

...Yunmelngen told me there's treasure buried five thousand meters below.

...And today is the ceremony to dig that final meter.

It was more or less a ribbon-cutting celebration. This event, which had been dubbed the Astral Power Festival of Spiritualism, would be starting at nine o'clock—in other words, that very moment. The miners would be on site as spectators. Writers had gathered from all over the world, and the event would likely be shown on TV as well. His sisters had been extra busy preparing for the spectacle.

"...I don't care about being on TV, but I guess it's something people would normally worry over."

"Thanks for waiting, Crow!"

"Let's get going! I'm going to look perfect if I make it on the screen!"

His twin sisters dashed right out of the house. They both wore modest clothes, but Eve applied a lipstick to look dressier, and Alicerose had wrapped a scarf around her neck.

"That's all you did?! You took an entire hour to put on some lipstick and wrap a scarf around your neck?!"

"We just haven't ever had to do this stuff before," Eve said.

"That's right, Crow," Alicerose agreed. "There are so many ways to tie a scarf."

"…Th-there are?"

They started walking down the main road.

The normally leisurely street was packed shoulder to shoulder that day. Usually, people would be working at this hour. Journalists, guards, and those carrying cameras stood out the most in the bustling street.

They eventually caught sight of a barricade and an even larger crowd. This was the entrance to the excavation site—the Planet's Navel.

"Oh, you three are late!" Musha, who had been standing in the audience, looked at them and waved. The rest of their coworkers were deeper in the crowd.

"Well, Alice just took so long getting ready," Eve said.

"I-it wasn't just me. You took your time, too!"

"Shush. His Excellency has appeared."

Drake had silenced the three girls and was pointing at the other side of the barricade. Their workplace, which they had normally entered and exited as they pleased based on recognition alone, was now surrounded by a ring of burly guards for VIPs.

At their center was a middle-aged man wearing a suit, who appeared amidst applause. He was tall, slim, and had sharp features. Lord Harkenweltz, who held supreme authority over the nation, passed in front of their eyes.

"Whoa! Is that actually His Excellency?! He glanced at us!"

"I-I feel like he met my eyes, too…!"

The twins were whispering to each other.

After all, to Imperial capital residents, seeing the Lord from this close was likely a once-in-a-lifetime event—if it even happened in one's lifetime at all.

The surrounding cameras and newspaper journalists' kept their eyes trained on that singular spot.

"...Oh."

Only Crossweil was looking away at the tagalong walking directly behind the Lord: the Crown Prince Yunmelngen, wearing a tidy white outfit. His eyes were charming, and bathed in sunlight, his blue hair glittered as it fluttered. The prince waved a hand at the crowd while walking by.

Then, in the next second, when their eyes met, the Crown Prince seemed to momentarily chuckle. Crossweil was positive only he had caught that laugh.

"...It's nice seeing His Excellency and all, but..." Eve clapped her hands together. "Hey, Crow, how long do you think we have to keep clapping?"

"It's about to start."

The guards surrounding the Lord and Crown Prince had walked up to the front of the lift.

A pedestal and button had been prepared there.

"That button's supposed to be connected to the drill down in the excavation area. The drill will started up once he presses it. Then we'll reach five thousand meters down."

"Oh? You sure know your stuff, Crow."

"I think I've just been paying more attention than you expected, Eve."

The Astral Power Festival of Spiritualism. In other words, this was the event where the Lord himself would reclaim the pool of new energy underneath the planet's surface.

"It's actually kind of unfair when you think about it," Eve said. She had stopped clapping before everyone else and crossed her arms. "It's the miners who dug this giant hole in the first place and got us down four thousand nine hundred ninety-nine meters, but then he gets the last most coveted meter? Am I right, Crow?"

"That's the whole reason why they gave us a bonus to make us feel better about it. "

"Oh, I see. Well, guess that's just how it is." She nodded, though reluctantly.

While the two of them were talking, the Lord and Crown Prince had finally placed their hands on the button. They had waited, idling as the cameras took their pictures.

"Please watch!"

"As His Excellency and His Highness the Crown Prince usher in a new era!"

They pressed the button, fanfare resounding all the while.

However...

That was it. At that very moment, the gigantic drill should have been boring into the planet below them at the excavation site. It would be eating through the hard bedrock, chiseling its way deeper, but of course, those on the surface couldn't have known of that.

A whole minute passed, then two.

"...This wasn't as exciting as I thought it'd be," Musha whispered.

"Yeah, and all they did was press one measly little button. I'm not that smart, so I don't know what's going on, but is that really it? Is it already coming out?"

No one responded. Not a single one of them had the answers. No one knew that the new energy—the astral power—from five thousand meters below the planet's surface was already surging up.

"..."

Then, right at that moment, single girl began to totter forward, wordlessly crossing the barricade and leaving behind the other spectators.

She was Eve Sophi Nebulis.

"Eve?! What's gotten into you?!" Crossweil shouted.

Eve did not respond. She didn't even turn back. Instead, she walked, her steps unstable, like a marionette being led toward the guards.

"...The voice...it calls......me......"

"Hm? What're you doing here, kid?"

"I know it's tempting to watch the ceremony from up close, but it's dangerous. You should wait back there."

The guards had noticed her. They tried to stop the small girl with their words.

"...Ugh...i-it hurts......stop..............don't...come into usssssssss!" Yunmelngen's cry also resounded throughout the space. The Crown Prince fell onto his knees, yelling and clawing at his head.

...Yunmelngen?!

...What's happening?!

There was clearly something wrong. Crossweil tried to call to the prince, but before he could, there was a shout.

"S-something is wrong down there?!"

That had come from one of the engineers. He had a comm pressed to his ear and was speaking to the other engineers, but because they were yelling, the audience was able to hear everything.

"A gigantic light burst from the five-thousand-meter point?! That must be the new energy! ...But you can't stop it from surging up? Then mobilize the defense wall!"

Though it was named astral energy, the new power source was still unidentified. In case it had an effect on the surface, the drill had been equipped with layers of alloy filters. The wall should have been able to withstand a surge from a large-scale geyser. However…

An explosive rumble came from below, shaking them.

"…What?" The engineer's voice was raspy as he continued. "……It passed the defensive wall and is still coming up?! Guh?!"

The next impact felt as though the very surface of the planet were being flipped over. The buildings quaked, the glass windows cracking. By the time they realized what was happening, the whole audience, Crossweil included, had been forced to their knees. Some had fallen onto their backs and hadn't been able to right themselves in the continued aftershocks.

What in the world had happened?

Or rather, what in the world was happening?

As Crossweil searched around, every single face was pale with one exception.

"……It calls…I am…being called……"

Standing past the barricade, Eve was staring down into the gigantic cavern, her eyes empty.

"Th-this is an emergency situation!"

An alert reverberated throughout the area.

"Please evacuate as quickly as possible. Try not to panic—"

It ended preemptively. The announcement and everything else were being hit with enough force to blast them away.

A torrent of vibrant light surged from five thousand meters below and was spouting from the gigantic opening. Like an immense geyser, it rose high into the air and created a rainbow-like arc.

It likely looked like a fantastical scene to those who saw it.

…Is this the new energy Yunmelngen told me about?

…This light?

That was the final scene that Crossweil Gate Nebulis saw before the entire world changed.

The light called astral power advanced toward the humans on the surface.

It surged through the twins, Crossweil's colleagues, the hundreds of spectators, and the Lord and the Crown Prince.

Crossweil lost consciousness as he was swallowed up in the eddy of light.

MEMORY ILLUMINATION 3

As Life Audibly Crumbled Apart

1

....

....

...What...was I doing again?

He opened his eyes.

He couldn't recall dreaming. He hadn't even remembered the moment he had closed his eyes as he looked up at a ceiling and realized he was on his back.

"...I......ouch!"

The moment he tried to rise from the pristine white sheets, he felt an acute pain from the back of his head.

He must have fallen backward and hit his head.

But if that were the case, when had that happened? And why?

"How are you feeling?" A nurse clad in white peeked in from the hallway.

"I'm glad. We thought you would wake soon," she continued. "I'll call the doctor. I think he'll probably examine you."

"..."

He realized he was at a hospital, and that he was being treated as a patient. Although his brain was hazy, he still had been able to understand.

"Can you remember your name?"

"...Crossweil Gate Nebulis," he answered.

"And what happened before you lost consciousness? Do you remember the explosion?"

An explosion? What explosion? Did it have anything to do with what he was doing here?

...I live in that junk house...

...I live there with my sisters. No, that wasn't it.

That wasn't the reason why he had fallen. He recalled he had left the house in the morning. He felt as though he'd headed to work as usual with his sisters.

...Wait, I didn't. We had the day off.

...Because we got to the goal, to five thousand meters.

All of the miners had been gathered by the opening.

"Oh!"

He remembered. He recalled the explosion.

"That's right! I was at...the Festival of Spiritualism! We were watching the moment when the astral power was being dug up, when the new energy was discovered. But then..."

Light had burst through. And that was all he remembered seeing. The colorful lights he had seen erupting from below the planet's surface had surged into the air like a geyser. The second he'd realized that, the light had also swallowed him.

"...I think I lost consciousness right after I got hit by that blast of light..."

"That is exactly right," the nurse slowly nodded. "Many people fainted from the blast. When we heard the news that hundreds of people lost consciousness all at once, we rushed over, but…luckily we found the cause was from momentary shock. It was just a bright light and a loud sound that caused it."

"So no one's…" Crossweil started to ask.

"The Imperial assembly announced to the rest of the world that they don't believe anyone will lose their life from this."

"…"

"Don't worry. The hospital agrees with the assessment, too."

She pointed around the room. There were three empty beds. It seemed he was the only one in the four-person room.

"The other three have already woken up and left," she told him.

"Has everyone left the hospital? Am I the last one…?"

"Yes. You've been here four days, Mr. Crossweil." She gave him a small smile. "Fifty-three people were brought to this hospital. Most of them woke the next day and were given a clean bill of health before leaving."

"…Um, do you happen to know where my sisters are?"

"What are their names?"

"Eve and Alicerose. They both have the last name Nebulis, like me."

"They've already been released," she said. Her reply was so quick, it was almost anticlimactic. She likely had been expecting him to ask about the others as soon as he woke, so she must have already looked into it ahead of time.

"…I'm glad," he said. "Just hearing that makes me feel so much better."

Deep within him, he wanted to ask what had happened to the Crown Prince as well, but stopped himself from asking.

…He wouldn't have been admitted to the same hospital anyway.

...And if I'm not careful about what I say, I might create trouble for him.

He was likely fine, too.

If anything had happened to the Lord or Crown Prince, there would have been a huge commotion. The patients likely wouldn't have been immediately discharged, either.

So he was glad.

It was nearly a miracle how no one had been victim to such a large explosion.

"May I ask a question?" he inquired. "Was the light we got showered in the new energy from the excavation site?"

"The Imperial assembly has announced it was, yes. They say that humanity has obtained a wonderful new resource."

"...Even though there was an accident?"

"Despite the explosion, there were no causalities. The reports say astral power is harmless to humans, which is great news."

"...I suppose so."

He couldn't argue with how she put it.

The light from the explosion.

Had that been fire or a heat wave with the same scope of impact, thousands would have become victim to the explosion. But no one had lost their lives. The intense light had simply showered them, and despite knocking them temporarily unconscious, it hadn't left a single wound on their bodies.

Astral power was harmless energy. That was likely better than the Empire could have ever imagined. The unprecedented accident had become a sort of advertisement for the other nations.

"I see," Crossweil said. "If my sisters have already been discharged, I guess I can leave without worrying too much about it."

"Just to warn you, you'll still need a thorough checkup before you can do that. You did hit your head when you fell, after all."

"Oh, right. I can still feel a bump on my head."

It still throbbed as well. He touched the back of his head automatically and brought his hand down to the back of his neck.

"Uh?"

Something felt off.

It didn't hurt or feel as if anything was there. But instinctively, he simply felt as though something was different.

"Um…do you have a mirror? Even a small handheld one."

He borrowed one used for examinations and checked the back of his neck. Something unfamiliar *was* there. At first glance, it looked like a birthmark. It was dark purple and spiral-shaped. Was it a bruise from when he had hit his head? Yet it was a very specific purple hue, and had a very specific shape.

…What is this?

…Did I injure this part when I fell?

It didn't hurt when he touched it.

"Oh?" The nurse peered at his neck and her eyes widened. "Looks like you have one too."

"……Huh?"

"Of the fifty-three brought in, about ten-odd people had a mark from where they hit themselves falling over. The Imperial assembly said they were forming a medical team to look into whether it has anything to do with the explosion. Do you feel any other symptoms around your bruise?"

"…No, not at all. Actually, my head hurts more."

It was a bruise? Were bruises ever this clear and distinct? And other people also had similar marks. Since there had to have been close to a thousand people caught in the blast, he wondered what had happened to the patients at other hospitals.

"You're not going to hold me until the mark goes away, are you…?" he asked.

"As long as your checkup looks fine, we'll schedule a follow-up, then you can go. Do you have any other questions?"

"...I don't."

"Then I'll head out. If anything happens, just let me know."

The nurse left, and he was alone in the four-person room.

"...What is this thing?"

He checked the mark on his neck again. Crossweil could think of only one reason for how he had developed it, and it was most likely due to the light of the astral power that had bathed him following the explosion.

...There's no way.

...The Imperial assembly officially announced astral power is harmless.

He felt slightly anxious.

He spent the rest of the evening with a nagging feeling in a corner of his mind, one that simply would not leave him.

The next day, after Crossweil finished his medical exam, he was allowed to leave without issue.

"Congrats on being discharged, Crow!"

"Took you long enough. You spent five whole days sleeping in the hospital, huh?"

It was the first time he was home in five days.

Crossweil was greeted by his sisters with the sweetest smile in the world and the most sardonic smirk ever.

"...You two are just way too different."

He had missed this.

Coming back to his normal life gave him relief.

"Looks like you both were discharged way before me," he said.

"Yes. I was discharged two days before you. Apparently Eve

woke up the same day as the blast and was walking around the hospital like nothing happened."

"That was quick!"

"...Heh," Eve gloated. "Unlike you, I'm not scrawny."

She sat cross-legged on the ground as she crossed her arms pridefully.

"It was a huge ordeal for me. Since I was one of the victims of the blast, I was surrounded by cameras the moment I left. They were making a whole commotion and prying about the light that showered us, and how I was feeling and stuff."

"Everyone must have rushed to you because you were the first one to wake up." Alicerose chuckled quietly.

When Crossweil looked at her kind eyes, he realized that they were bloodshot.

"Alice, your eyes look irritated," he said.

"Oh, you mean this? ...Yeah, I haven't slept well for the last three days." She held her hands up to her eyes and laughed bashfully. "But it's not a big deal. You're so sweet, Crow, thank you for worrying about me. I'm sure I'll feel better soon enough."

"...You haven't been sleeping?"

"I just haven't been able to fall asleep. It's been so hot the last few days."

She turned her eyes away. He didn't press her about it any further. He couldn't when his kind sister was acting like that.

"Hey, Crow, so I bet you wanna get a look at my eyes too, huh," Eve said.

"...Uh, well, if Alice isn't feeling sleepy, then I just would assume you're fine too, Eve. You really do seem okay, actually."

"..."

Eve widened her eyes as she stared at him seriously. For a

moment, she just blinked, as though she wasn't sure he'd actually addressed her.

"What gives you the right to be so cheeky, Crow?!"

"Ouch?!"

She had punched him.

For some reason, she'd hit him even though he'd been worried about how his sisters were doing.

"I'm saying you should worry more about yourself than me," Eve said. "Sheesh. Unlike you and Alice, I'm not frail. Never even caught a cold."

Hmph, Eve sighed as she crossed her arms again.

"It's almost time for the sale at the supermarket. I'll go so you and Alice wait here at home."

"Oh, Eve, in that case, let me—" Alicerose tried to volunteer herself.

"I'll be fine going alone," she didn't even let her sister finish her sentence. "All right? If you really haven't been sleeping, then you should rest. Same goes for you, Crow. What'll we do if you two overdo it and faint again right after getting out of the hospital?"

"…"

"…"

As Eve said that, Crossweil and Alicerose turned to look at one another.

"Hm? What's up? Why're you acting like that?"

"Nah, no reason," Crossweil responded.

"I really love how you act like such a little kid sometimes, Eve," Alice said.

"Wh-who are you calling a little kid?! I obviously act like the older sister! Alice, stop grinning like that! …Ugh, who cares!"

Eve rushed out of the house, her face bright red. Both Crossweil and Alicerose watched her adorable retreating back. Yes, despite the explosion of light, they would continue living their lives as usual.

Crossweil never so much as doubted that.

For the time being.

2

Night wore on.

The blue sky darkened as the curtain of night fell over it in those early hours of evening. One house at a time, the lights on the capital streets went out.

The sound of the cars on the roads, once bustling, subsided.

Not even the cries of a bird or the calls of the insects could be heard.

In the dead of night, as the people of the capital slept—no, as the capital itself slumbered...

...What is this?

A faint noise had woken Crossweil.

A rustle, to be more precise.

Then he heard someone tumble onto the floor and groan in a stifled voice.

That was...

It was coming from the person sleeping right beside him.

"...Ah...uh......ugh...n-no...hot......stop......"

Was it Alice? He could hardly make anything out in the

pitch-black living room, but he could still hear his sister's pain as she slept next to him. He held his breath and focused on the darkness just centimeters before his eyes.

But he hadn't needed to do that.

Bwoosht!

Right in front of his eyes, he saw hazy light emanating from his sister's body.

"Alice?!"

"……Ugh……Cr…ow…" She turned to him, looking pallid.

He found that she had abandoned her nightclothes and was now in only her undergarments. Beads of sweat rolled down her neck and back like a waterfall.

"Alice?!" he called her again. "What's wrong?!"

"……Crow…" Her breath ran ragged as she breathed, and her wet eyes turned to him.

"I feel…hot……," she said.

"Is it a cold?"

"No…not like that…it's like magma is deep inside me. I feel like the heat could scald me…"

"What?"

He tried to remember their conversation from earlier that day.

"Alice, your eyes look red."

"Oh, you mean this? …Yeah, I haven't slept well for the last three days."

So this was the reason she hadn't been sleeping.

"What's been making you feel too hot to sleep, Alice?! Since when?!"

"…"

"We need to get you to the hospital right now!"

He grabbed her arm.

Even though she had barely been able to speak or breathe, his sister grabbed his wrist, her desperation showing on her face. She was telling him not to—hinting she didn't want to go. But why was that?

He found the answer on her left shoulder.

"...Huh? What is that?!"

A green mark shone on her shoulder. The faint light in the room was coming from none other than that.

...It's the same as the one on my neck!

...Wait, it isn't. Mine is purple, but hers is green.

The shape was different as well. His mark formed a spiral, but hers looked more like a rounded heart.

...Alice has a mark, not just me.

...Wait, then does Eve have one too?

"Eve! This is serious. Alice is—"

But he stopped in his tracks.

Why hadn't Eve woken up?

They'd been talking in such loud voices that it was odd she hadn't reacted at all. There was no way she couldn't have noticed her little sister in such agony night after night.

"It's calling."

He heard a voice, one with the vestiges of childishness to it.

He turned to find the curtains wide open. The moonlight filtered in and illuminated by it, he found a girl, tanned from the sun, standing there.

"Eve?"

"…" She didn't answer. Had she not heard him?

Eve stared outside, her eyes wide open. Then she suddenly moved. Her nightclothes were thin, and her feet were bare, yet she leapt out the open window and began to walk with a purpose down the main street.

"Hey, where do you think you're going, Eve! Don't you see how much pain Alice is in?!"

She didn't reply.

As he watched her leave, he felt a chill run down his spine.

A dark mark. Under the thin fabric of her nightclothes, he saw the faint glow of a dark mark on her body. It was large, almost as though swallowing her entire back.

…*Eve has a mark on her back, too.*

…*What is it? What's happening?!*

His instincts told him what it was.

This was all happening because of the marks. Alicerose was burning up as though she had a fever, and Eve was acting like a puppet without her own will all because of them.

…*Will this happen to me too?*

…*No, this isn't the time to think about that!*

He needed to help both his fever-stricken sister and Eve, who had leapt out of the window under a will that was not her own. But he could only save one of them. Which one should he prioritize?

"Huh! …Sorry, Alice, but I'll be back in ten!"

He laid her down as she breathed raggedly.

He needed to help the older twin first.

…*The mark on Eve's back stands out way more than either Alice's or mine.*

…*There'd be a scene if anyone else sees it.*

No one would have believed in a birthmark that could glow in the night. He was sure that a stranger would find it ominous. And because they'd already been involved in the accident from five days ago, it was likely result in more trouble for them.

"Ugh, what's going on?!"

He didn't even have time to change.

He put a jacket on over his own nightclothes and rushed out barely dressed.

Where was she? Where had she gone?

"Over there!"

In the dark of night, he could barely make out the silver-haired girl lit by the dim streetlights.

As the cold wind lashed about, he ran after her small figure. It gave him a feeling of déjà vu. This was the same main road he would travel down during the day. The hospital he had been admitted to was up ahead, and on the way was—

"She couldn't possibly be?!"

He knew where she was going. They were headed to the site of the explosion that had been responsible for the mysterious marks that had appeared on all three of them.

"The Planet's Navel!"

The place was now surrounded by two or three layers of barricades, which was only natural given the size of the blast. With the possibility of a second upsurge of energy, countermeasures had been taken to ward off any would-be visitors.

However...

The steel netting and wires had been torn to shreds.

"......Huh?"

The alloy wires should have been impenetrable except by specialized tools. In fact, even the security camera cables seemed to have been melted into a dribbling mush from intense heat, and had also been wrenched apart.

The same was true of the steel mesh.

And the size of the holes left behind were oddly perfect for a small girl to travel through.

…Wait…this can't be real.

…Eve couldn't have…not this…

This wasn't the work of any human.

How had she torn through the alloy, much less melted it?

And…

…there Eve was, standing before the gigantic opening the light had burst out from.

The moonlight shone down upon her, illuminating the large mark on her skin. Her fair hair twinkled in the light as it fluttered. She was peering into the open hole.

"Eve, it's me!"

He didn't know if his sister had heard him, but as he was now, there was nothing else he could do but call out to her.

"I'll tell you as many times as I need to: Alice is in trouble. You need to come back home with me right now!"

"…"

"Please, Eve!"

"Who?"

"What?" he responded.

Who are you? Somewhere inside him, he had been ready for his sister to ask him that. But the words that came from her mouth were even more inexplicable than he had imagined.

"Who am I?" she asked.

"……Huh? Come on, what are you saying? Eve?!"

"Wh…what am I…h-human…or astral power…?"

Her delicate limbs began to shiver. She held her head and doubled over.

"...I...I'm......"

The mark beneath her thin clothes began to glow even stronger. The light swelled, just as it had during the eruption. A torrent of light rivaling the explosion from five days ago came flooding out of her.

"What?!"

That decided it. What he was witnessing—human flesh releasing an inordinate amount of light—was nothing short of unnatural.

... *This isn't any ordinary mark.*

... *There's something going awry in our bodies. The marks are a sign of abnormality!*

Eve's mark was bigger than anyone else's, which must have influenced her behavior as well. But what could he do?

"...Cr...ow...run away...!"

"What?!"

"A-ahhhh!"

He wondered how her small frame was even capable of making such a loud noise. After shouting at him, Eve Sophi Nebulis shrieked.

Her entire body released rays of light several hundred times stronger than before.

But there was no sound now.

A beam that had just grazed Crossweil's face pierced through a metal rod, evaporating it without a trace. The light flew upward, toward the clouds, blasting them away upon contact.

"......You've gotta be kidding me."

He couldn't fathom how hot the light must have been to have punctured the thick rod. In addition to that, he'd seen hundreds of rays bursting from her. He was relieved many of them had shot up into the sky, but if the light came back down to earth, the entire capital block likely would have been obliterated.

"......Crow...help me..."

"...Eve?"

The small girl was right before his eyes. She knelt in front of him, squeezing the hem of her clothes in her hands, as she looked up at him weakly, almost as though begging.

"...I don't...want this......"

She slowly crumpled. His sister lost consciousness, still clutching at her clothes.

3

The next morning.

Crossweil was at a loss for words when he heard his sisters' responses to his questions.

"What? What are you even talking about, Crow? You think I jumped out the window?"

"And I was groaning during the night? ...I'm sorry. I don't remember any of it."

They didn't remember a thing. In fact, they were questioning the idea that something had happened last night. The two seemed to simply think they hadn't gotten enough sleep.

...But Alice looked like she was in so much pain.

...How can Eve not remember anything about what happened at the excavation site?

Their memories were simply...missing.

Should he have called in a doctor right away? They had both undergone full physicals just days before and been declared free of any abnormalities. He doubted any hospital would be able to uncover the mystery of what was going on.

...The cause is easy to see.

...After the light from the blast showered us, the people around developed strange marks and have started to act oddly.

The marks glowed faintly as well. And not a single one was the same, in shape or color

"Hey, Crow, why're you so quiet?" Eve gave him a smack on the back. She was overflowing with cheer, as though the entire ordeal the night before and her confusion had never happened. "Are you still thinking about the blast?"

"...To be honest, I am."

"You are? I think finding a new workplace is more important to us right now, though."

The job at the Planet's Navel had concluded. Their miner friends had scattered to the four winds and would likely seek new work in the capital.

"...Eve, can I turn on the TV?"

"All the channels are gonna be covering the explosion, just so you know."

"That's what I want to see," he replied.

"They just keep reporting the same information over again without giving any more. Well, it's not like we've got anything better to do."

He turned on the TV in the corner.

When he'd been admitted into the hospital, and the day after, the news had only featured the blast. And just like Eve had said, there wasn't any new information to be found.

...I want to know more about the marks.

...Just like me, there have got to be people wondering what's going on.

He stared at the TV, unblinking.

"We have a follow-up report on the fifty-fourth excavation point's blast."

"At site of the explosion, also known as the Planet's Navel, they were excavating for a new form of energy below the planet's surface. The incident itself occurred during a formal ceremony."

"According to the Imperial assembly, the new energy erupted from underground—"

"Specialists are calling this an inexplicable power vortex."

"Seven hundred eighty-four people were involved in the incident. We have just confirmed that all affected people have been discharged from the hospital. The incident was not life-threatening."

"See?" Eve said. "None of it's interesting."

She sighed as she lay on the ground. "What kind of name is 'vortex' anyway? I don't care about naming the blast. We've got our hands full just trying to find work."

"Still, it's good that everyone is safe," Alicerose said, seeming genuinely relieved. "The explosion sure seemed big, but it was really the light and sound that was making it seem flashy. So they're calling it astral power? I'm so glad the energy is harmless."

Harmless? Was it really, though?

"..." He felt the back of his neck as casually as he could, without letting his sisters notice.

It was where his mark was. Nothing about it seemed odd as he touched it. It wasn't painful in the slightest. He only got a strange sense that he knew it was there.

"Up next, we have some new information! We have new footage, fresh from last night, to showcase it!"

New footage from last night?

When he heard that, he turned to look at Eve before he'd even realized what he was doing.

Had someone seen what had happened last night? No, if they had, the press and police would have been forcing their way into their home by now.

"This footage is of a fourteen-year-old girl who worked at the fifty-fourth excavation point. She was exposed to the light of the vortex and had been admitted to the hospital and was discharged just recently."

The girl seemed to have the same build as Eve. Her hair was curled in ringlets and was a characteristic brown. She seemed nervous in front of the camera, trying to make herself look smaller in what was likely her first time in the spotlight.

"Oh, is that Musha?"

"That's Musha!"

Alicerose and Eve widened their eyes.

Their coworker was on TV. She had been swept up in the vortex too and likely had been treated at another hospital.

"Why is she on TV...?" Eve trained her eyes on the screen.

Musha opened up her palm to show it to the camera. There was a red mark. The same as theirs. The truly surprising event occurred next.

Crimson flames burst from her palm.

"What?!"

"...Huh?"

"Whaaat?! Wh-what was that just now?! What kind of trick was that?!"

Eve started to shout at the TV.

Viewers all over the world likely felt the same as she was now, wondering what kind of trick they had just witnessed.

"This is no trick or chemical reaction, folks."

"Some of those who were admitted to hospitals during the vortex have developed these marks. They were exposed to the new energy called astral power!"

Finally...

"..."

Cold sweat trickled down Crossweil's cheek. Finally, there were others who were taking notice of the marks. He had also seen that those affected were displaying abnormal powers, just as Eve had demonstrated the night before.

...If Musha is affected too, then it's not just the three of us.

...It's everyone who was at that place.

This had finally been broadcasted to the world.

"H-hey, Alice, let me see your shoulder!" Eve insisted.

"Eep?!"

Eve tugged at her sister's shirt and checked Alicerose's shoulder. Her mark looked different from Musha's.

"...Alice, can you do that thing, too?"

"O-of course not!"

She shook her head insistently.

"What about you, Eve?!"

"Ack! Stop that, Alice!"

This time the younger sibling did her inspection. She lifted her sister's shirt, showing a rather bold amount of skin. Then she stared at the dark mark covering almost the entirety of Eve's back.

"...Eve, your mark is kind of big."

"S-so what! I couldn't control that. It formed on its own. But I can't do that thing Musha did!"

Eve was half right and half wrong.

It was possible she couldn't produce flames. But last night, her whole body had glowed, and Crossweil had witnessed her releasing several hundred rays of intense light. Her powers were on an entirely different scale compared to Musha's.

"...What are these marks...?" Alicerose murmured as she placed a hand on her shoulder. "...Eve."

"How should I know?! I just told you. We didn't have any control over them. The doctors or researchers or whoever can figure it out!" Eve almost seemed combative. "We should be focusing on finding our next jobs. That's the only thing that needs to be on your mind!"

However...

Society did not agree.

The TV programs started the next day. Dozens of newspaper reporters and TV news crews appeared, pressing those caught in the vortex to come forward if they had also developed marks.

That continued each day, and they would be surrounded by numerous reporting crews by simply walking out their door.

"Damn it! Cut that out! I'm not something to gawk at!"

Eve, of course, did not hide her chagrin.

Even Alicerose's health began to crumble as the world turned its eyes on her.

"Eve... Do you think we can ask them to just stop coming?" Alicerose inquired.

"You idiot! As soon as we show our faces, they'll start

broadcasting us. Those journalists couldn't care less about how we're feeling!"

They were as good as prisoners in their own home, surveilled twenty-four seven. Their daily routines were disrupted, and they weren't able to go grocery shopping.

How could they fix this? How could they stop the TV programs and reporters and return to their normal lives? Every day and every night, Crossweil lost sleep from thinking of a solution.

"...He's the answer."

He recalled the friendly smile of his so-called conversation partner. The Crown Prince Yunmelngen. Because the prince had also been caught up in the vortex, he had to already have more information than anyone.

...Was he hospitalized like us?

...I've been wondering how he's been doing. I haven't heard anything about the prince...

...and he wasn't to contact the prince himself.

But considering the situation, this had to be an exception.

"Yunmelngen! Please, pick up!"

He gripped the comm, as though grasping at straws, but it rang dozens of times without an answer.

"Right, I guess that's it. He must be busy......but like I'll stop there!"

He could only put up with so much. He was at his limit. The older twin was looking stressed, and the younger twin was bedridden. To deal with the situation, he'd need Yunmelngen's help.

"You told me I could use it whenever I want!"

He would go meet the prince using the secret passageway that connected to the Lord's residence.

4

The Castle Tower Seat.

The Lord's residence could only be entered by a small number of important Imperial personages, after going through extensive identity checks. Crossweil passed through undetected by the guards or surveillance.

"…Even though it's my second time coming here, I'm still nervous."

Crossweil looked up at the glittering stained glass in the beautiful hallway. It looked exactly as it had the first time. The hallway was spacious and long enough to hold a footrace. People who looked like guards periodically passed through it as well.

Then he arrived at a gigantic door decorated in gilt designs. This was, of course, the entrance to Yunmelngen's chambers. Naturally the door could not be opened from the outside. He needed to find a way to have Yunmelngen open it from within.

"…But he won't answer me." He hadn't gotten a response on the comm. "Hey, Yunmelngen! I know you're in there!"

Though he knew the risks of the passing guards hearing him, he yelled.

Next, he knocked.

He was here. Attempting to tell the prince that, he tried again and again, hitting the door and calling Yunmelngen's name.

…*I'll never get an answer like this.*

…*He won't pick up his comm. Maybe he's still hospitalized somewhere?*

In that case, Crossweil would have to give up. Though he had made it this far, there was a possibility that the Crown Prince wasn't here.

"Damn it. If you're not there, at least tell me…!"

As a last resort, he pushed the door as hard as he could.

He had to crane his neck to look up at the imposing mecha-nized door. It was impossible to open with human strength. Even a large truck on a collision course toward it likely wouldn't have made it budge an inch. Crossweil knew that.

He knew it, but…

So E lu emne xel noi Es—accept me.

Someone had whispered.

Whose voice had that been? He hadn't even had time to won-der as a dazzling light flashed. It had come from his purple mark.

"…Is that my mark?!"

The light before his eyes was surging from the back of his own neck. Upon realizing that, something strange happened.

Creak.

The door he had been pushing against creaked at its joints as it slowly started to open.

"……What?!"

He was opening it with pure brute-force. This door to the Crown Prince's room, that wouldn't have budged even if dozens of people pushed against it, had opened.

…What's going on with my arms?

…Is that thing happening to me, too?!

It seemed he also had paranormal abilities. He had just been late to notice them. He simply hadn't realized because they weren't as easy to see as Musha's flames or Eve's flashes of light.

"…What's going on…with me……?"

But he had to figure that out later. He quickly snuck through the gap in the door, heading into the extravagant chambers that reminded him of what a suite room supposedly looked like.

"Yunmelngen! Are you here?!"

"........Crow?"

The voice was incredibly feeble. It had come from the corner of the spacious room, from the canopied bed.

"I'm so glad you're here, Yunmelngen. Sorry I barged my way in, but the capital's been a mess. Me and my family have been, too. I wanted to see if you knew any—"

"Stay back!"

"Uh?"

"Don't come near me... You can't... Please don't look."

Don't look. He was so taken aback by the unfamiliar words that he stared at the bed unconsciously. He made out a figure through the thin transparent curtains. Someone was under the blankets. Or rather, something?

A gigantic silver tail had fallen out from under the covers.

Was there an animal on the bed? It was too big to be a cat's, and he could hardly think a fox would be in this room. Now that he thought of it, where was the Crown Prince?

"Where are you, Yunmelngen?"

"............"

"Is that your pet on the bed? I can't tell if it's a fox or a cat."

"Tsk."

In that moment, the bulge under the blankets shifted. The beast had twitched.

"Hey, Yunmelngen?"

A short period of silence was shared between them.

"......**We never should have touched it.**" Crossweil heard Yunmelngen's voice from the bed. **"It was not energy that erupted from the core of the planet. It was tens of thousands, hundreds of millions of astral powers, each with their own will. They possessed the humans. Their power is so strong that once they fully fuse with a person, they can no longer remain human."**

"Hm?"

What did that mean?

The eruption hadn't been from energy? And what did it mean that astral powers possess people?

"...You stop being human once that happens."

"Hey, Yunmelngen, what are you—"

"Like me."

The blankets flew away.

Crossweil gaze at them as they sailed through the air, and suddenly, he felt an intense pain from his neck and back. He almost blacked out.

"...Guh?!"

Before he even realized what was happening, he had been grabbed by the neck and slammed against the wall.

"Ha-ha!"

"You're?!"

He could see the vestiges of Yunmelngen's features on the face, but the thing that was holding him by the neck was most certainly a monster. The prince's beautiful blue hair had been replaced by thick silver hair and fur, which covered the creature's whole body. His fingertips were ferocious claws and equally fierce fangs peeked from his mouth. He even had a tail.

He looked like a beastperson from a fairy tale, if not a monster.

"Looks like I've found myself a human. Won't you play with Meln?" the thing that had once been Yunmelngen asked.

He no longer addressed himself with the royal "we." And Crow was now just a "human."

"You?!"

"I am Meln. What you get when you throw a human being and astral power together."

Crossweil felt the beast's grip tighten around his throat.

Even the wall was beginning to crack, unable to withstand the strain of having Crossweil being pushed against it. Normal human bones would have crumbled under such pressure. Their bodies would have been crushed as well. The unnatural power inside him had saved him.

"Ha-ha. Sturdy, aren't you, human?"

"…Yeah, I am! But not by choice!"

He grabbed the hand on his throat.

"This is starting to get on my nerves, too. I don't get what's happening!"

Somewhere in his heart, he had been prepared for this. He had seen the changes in his sisters. And even how there was something odd about him.

…I knew he wouldn't be any exception.

…Since he was in the middle of the blast. I thought something was up!

He'd already expected it. That was why he'd been able to keep his composure—just barely—even in this situation.

"Open up your eyes already!"

He pulled the wrist he held up and flung the arm away as hard as he could toward the floor. Before hitting the floor, the beast had nimbly flipped backward like a cat. It landed easily and leapt at Crossweil again. It flashed its claws, sharp as knifepoints.

"Give it to me."

The claws stopped just as they were about to reach Crossweil. "Yunmelngen?"

"...This body...we...Meln is...we...Meln..."

The creature stopped. He fell to his knees, held his own head, and began to shiver.

What in the world had happened?

Crossweil watched, half-thunderstruck.

".........Crow..." The beast still clutched his head as his voice rasped.

He'd said "Crow." Not "human" like earlier. Yunmelngen had used Crossweil's usual nickname.

"...Close...the door..."

"Huh? Okay!" He quickly did as instructed before guards came rushing in from the noise.

"......It's okay... It should be okay for a while..."

The Crown Prince raised his head while still sitting on the ground. He looked at Crossweil's red neck, then at his own beast-like body that had inflicted the damage.

"...We...don't know what to say anymore...sorry, Crow...," Yunmelngen said, sounding close to tears. **"Look at this body...it must look horrible to you...these claws and fangs... The fur all over... It all happened overnight."**

"Yunmelngen."

"...What is it?"

"I think you know the most about what's happened." He got straight to the point and stopped Yunmelngen from disparaging himself. "It's not just you. Hundreds of people are going through this. Me and my family, too. And my coworkers from the excavation site."

"............."

"So I came here to talk to you. I want to try to figure out where to move forward from here."

"...You're so easygoing, Crow."

The beast weakly gave him a bitter smile.

"But you see the situation. This might call for a little more panic and inner turmoil, don't you think?"

"I did panic, and I went through plenty of turmoil already. I'm already emotionally numb to what's going on."

"...Well, I'm just happy you don't hate me after seeing me like this."

Yunmelngen stroked his ears, which poked out from atop his head. His expression softened.

"You came all the way here, after all. Then I suppose I have to humor you. But I'd like to ask for something first..."

"What?"

"...Um...don't stare like that...I'll put on some clothes..."

Crossweil finally realized Yunmelngen wasn't wearing anything. In human terms, the Crown Prince would have been nude. However, Crossweil had barely registered that because the prince was covered in fur from head to toe.

"Do you really need clothes?"

"You nitwit!" Yunmelngen scolded him.

Once the prince was clothed, they began to talk.

"That day, the humans around the Planet's Navel were

possessed by astral powers. Many of them are asymptomatic like you."

"Asymptomatic, my butt. My neck has got—"

"The astral crest is nothing but a mark. It has no ill effects."

"What's an astral crest?"

"The mark on the back of your neck. It is proof that you have astral power in you, but as long as it doesn't hurt, it's asymptomatic. But there were some that were not well-meaning."

The Lord was still comatose. Yunmelngen's very body had been transformed. He had been out of his mind fighting the astral power within him that he hadn't been able to even respond on his comm.

"No two astral powers are alike. And Meln happened to get the worst one."

"Hey."

He tensed up unconsciously. Yunmelngen had stopped using the royal "we" and was back to using "Meln" again. Was he in for another attack like earlier?

"We're fused together," Yunmelngen sat cross-legged and said with a self-derisive smile. **"I think I won't lose my senses and become violent again like earlier…but I think Meln will be like this forever."**

"You mean in that form?"

"I don't find it disagreeable. I've started to think it's fine. I think the fusion between my human side and the astral power has come that far along. I don't even have the same human sense of self."

It wasn't just his body that was changing, but also his mentality. Crossweil recalled someone else with similar symptoms.

"…I think Eve might be in a similar situation as you."

She would lose her sense of self before going off somewhere. She had an extra-large mark on her back and had demonstrated power on par with a weapon. In terms of destructive strength, she likely had more potential than Yunmelngen.

"I need to at least keep Eve a secret somehow. Because of Musha, journalists are going to keep coming to the capital from all over the world."

"You can't stop that."

"...You're quick to assume."

"That's why I was hiding in my room. Your family's only option is to lie low."

Even the Crown Prince couldn't control what was happening. Even if he could stop the press within the Empire, he couldn't do anything about those from outside.

"I suspect there will only be more people possessed by the astral powers. I think we'll discover many, many more."

"There were only supposed to be about eight hundred people in the hospital, though."

"That's only the audience at the Planet's Navel. Remember, the astral powers' light flew up into the sky of the capital."

"...Which means?"

"They covered the entire capital."

Tens of thousands had been exposed to it. A fraction of them would develop marks and would likely find themselves with powers. They just had yet to realize it.

...Or they're hiding it.

...They might be scared of what's happening, like me and my sisters.

The true chaos would begin after this.

Because of what had happened with Musha, the whole world had taken notice of astral power.

"What happens to us if the commotion spreads?"

"————" Yunmelngen looked at the ceiling. As Crossweil watched the prince, a long silence followed.

"There are two possibilities. If things go well, the spotlight will be given to those with abilities from astral powers. If not..."

"Then what?"

"We'll likely be feared as monsters."

For the first few weeks, Yunmelngen's best-case scenario held true.

Other people like Musha showed off their miraculous powers, and TV and newspaper journalists spread the word on a grander scale.

They began to call the marks astral crests. Some even started to call them the "chosen ones"—stars.

But a month after the events, ominous clouds began to gather steadily within the Empire.

People with astral powers were labeled as violent and prone to crime.

A case of a girl setting a group of men ablaze because she hadn't "cared for" them changed things.

As did the robberies in which someone used an astral power to steal valuables from homes.

"...There were only three cases last week," Crossweil said. "But this week it reached eleven. They put us up on a pedestal on TV at the beginning, but now they're calling us astral power contaminators. *Contaminators*...have you ever heard anything worse?"

"People who receive astral power change, after all. How they think and how they act will be influenced." Yunmelngen's voice came from the comm. **"Say you were to find yourself with enough**

money to spend on anything for a lifetime. Most humans would abandon their jobs or stop going to school."

"Are you saying it's the same thing as having money?"

"Astral powers can be more malignant," Yunmelngen said, sounding philosophical. "They can get revenge."

"Revenge?"

"For example, what would happen if a child with astral powers had been bullied at school? They likely would try to get revenge on their bullies. And their powers would be perfect for doing it."

" ... "

"There are other examples, too. Other reasons, such as poverty and misfortune that have made a great number of humans feel ostracized by society and hold a grudge against the world. And a fraction of those people have obtained the power to release their pent-up frustrations."

Astral power was awe-inspiring. Though the powers that each person obtained varied, to an ordinary person, each power was far more threatening than any gun. Crossweil had seen guards on patrol multiple times, seemingly wary of the astral power contaminators.

"But only a few people are abusing their powers...," Crossweil said.

He and his sisters weren't. His coworkers weren't, either. Since seeing the signs of the tide turning against those with astral power, he had been doing everything he could to live a quiet life with bated breath.

"Have you heard the phrase 'bad money drives out good'? The bad actors are the ones who are most noticed."

" ... "

"I am working as well, of course. While the Lord has yet to wake, the Eight Great Elders lead the Imperial assembly. Though it pains me to admit this, I've asked them for help. I've told them those contaminated by astral power were the victims of the event, and to stop the unfounded rumors from circulating."

"Thank you" was all Crossweil said.

"It's not as effective as you'd think, though. The Eight Great Elders are not to be trusted."

"What?"

"I can't let myself be seen in public in this form. The Eight Great Elders are the only people who can do anything about the situation, but…"

The prince wasn't being clear. There was something troubling him, which was unusual.

"I don't like them. The Lord changed after welcoming them in."

———————

The small room was dim—very dim.

A secret underground audience chamber below the Imperial assembly.

And there, in that very space…

The eight men and women known as the sages of the Empire sat facing one another.

"The astral power exists."

"The legends passed down by the Astrals were true. We have obtained a new energy that will re-create the world."

"Things have progressed well to this point. The issue now is—"

"We never could have guessed the power would have such a great affinity that it would possess humans..."

The powerful energy was enough to revolutionize the age they lived in. However, the Eight Great Elders had not anticipated that the power would dwell in people.

"What a troubling divergence from the plan..."

"Yes. We reviewed so many possibilities, yet reality far exceeded our expectations."

The astral power eruption had been like a volcano. During the Festival of Spiritualism, the enormous amount of energy had mercilessly scorched its surroundings like lava. Even the Lord and Crown Prince had been helplessly swallowed up in the deluge.

Their plans gone awry.

"The Crown Prince survived."

The astral powers evolved mankind.

The Eight Great Elders could not have foreseen that the powers would take refuge in humans.

Powers that could create windstorms, summon enough fire to engulf a building, and freeze a tank. The birth of individuals with so much power had disrupted the world's power balance.

"It seems the astral powers differ greatly."

"We only understand a small sample size. It is likely even more of those with power that far exceed our postulations will turn up... Now the issue we face is what to do with them."

"The Crown Prince."

"The astral power that took possession of that thing must have likely been closest to the planet's core."

And that hadn't been in the plans. The Crown Prince, who

should have been eliminated by the blast of energy, had instead transcended humanity and been reborn.

"The Crown Prince seems to have suspicions."

"But does not lay a finger on the Eight Great Elders. The prince's monstrous appearance has rendered them unable to dream of leaving the Castle Tower Seat. And they are still but a child."

"We hold the Empire in our hands."

"The astral power contaminators are sure to gain power in the future. We must act before that. 'Contaminators' is such a weak word. We should find a name with a more menacing ring to it in advance."

"..."

"..."

Silence fell over the room.

The eight sages watched each other, still quiet.

"Witch."

"It is decided. We will call those who have astral powers witches and sorcerers. We will forbid all other names within the Imperial territories from being used."

"Luclezeus, how many crimes have been committed by the mages and sorcerers within the Empire?"

"Eleven."

"Not nearly enough. That will not change the world's view of them."

"Then let us increase the number."

5

Life continued, living hidden indoors with bated breath. Outside the open curtains, the reporters and journalists were still likely flocking around the vicinity looking for someone to hound. Crossweil, Eve, and Alicerose were not exempt from this.

Overcome by the stifling atmosphere, they steadily spoke less to each other. When they did, everything they talked about was cheerless.

How many days had it been? They turned off the lights in the room and absentmindedly watched the TV reports each day. But today, of all days, they had a visitor.

"I'm sorry!" The sobs of a small girl shook their small house. "...If...if I just hadn't gone on TV...!"

It was Musha.

She wiped her eyes with her right hand, where a red mark glittered. That mark had the power to produce flames, and that news had spread worldwide like wildfire.

"I was so worried about it at first that I went to the hospital," she said. "But then TV reporters found me and said all sorts of nice things about how I had an amazing power...no one had said anything nice like that to me before and I was so happy that I went on TV..."

"None of this is your fault," Eve said from the floor, spitting the words out.

She pointed at the TV in the corner of the room.

"Look at the news. It's another witch with the beast's mark. She's rampaging around the Empire creating more problems. I don't know what kind of idiot she is, but she's the reason why the public hates us."

There were an endless number of people using their astral powers for crimes and in acts of violence. There had only been eleven last week. Now this week there were suddenly a hundred twelve incidents. They were growing exponentially.

"You made it out of your home, but ours is being regularly watched by the guards. That's how it is everywhere."

Public opinion had changed. The "stars" with the miraculous powers were now dangerous people worthy of surveillance.

"There was another report about a witch who got caught," Alicerose suddenly said.

Her face was clouded over as she watched the TV. He hadn't seen his sister's sweet and cheerful smile in days.

"Anna from next door wouldn't even talk to me when I went out for groceries yesterday."

"Nobody would want to talk to us right now. The TV and newspapers treat us like a gang. Hey, Crow, don't be so quiet and join the conversation, will ya?"

"..."

"Hey, Crow?"

".......Ugh. Yeah, I'm listening," he said. When Eve turned to him and called his name, Crossweil quickly nodded.

"I was too focused on the TV," he explained.

That was half-true. He'd been watching TV but focused on something else.

...What's going on, Yunmelngen?

...You told me you were trying to keep public opinion of astral power contaminators from falling!

But this was their reality.

The TV reports and news articles were behaving with a strange amount of caution toward them, even deriding them as witches and wizards without batting an eye.

Armed forces surrounded their homes, and they were spied on even while buying their groceries.

...There are astral power contaminators willing to commit acts of violence.

...Even if that's the case, how could there be so many new crimes? Are these numbers real?

In the very least, Crossweil had yet to see a crime in his area that actually involved astral power.

...If I could just get in contact with Yunmelngen again.

...And if he could pull himself together.

He hadn't gotten a response back from the Crown Prince. When he had last gotten in touch days ago, he'd learned that the changes Yunmelngen was going through were ongoing and that the prince was still sometimes losing consciousness.

"...I'll go home," Musha said, standing up. "The military police outside must have followed me from home, so I'm just creating trouble for you by being here..."

"Hey, wait, Musha! You leaving won't change anything!"

"Th-that's right, Musha. We're all uneasy. We'll feel better if we're together!"

Eve and Alicerose leapt up. But it wasn't them that Musha looked at.

"Crow." Instead, she addressed him. "You're a boy. Make sure to protect your sisters."

"Huh!"

"See ya!"

She opened the door and ran outside. She pushed through the ring of military police and camera-wielding media as she sprinted down the main road without turning back.

"Musha..." Alicerose said.

"She's the youngest out of us, but she's trying to make us feel better." Eve gritted her teeth. Even Eve, who normally laughed everything off, seemed to have trouble figuring out what to say.

"How did this happen…?" she murmured, leaning against a wall. "We haven't done anything, but the whole world is calling us witches, and guards are surveilling and arresting us now. Why? If they're doing everything they can to detain us, then…we should rebel like the witches they think we are—"

"Eve," Alicerose said.

"I'm kidding. Obviously it was a joke." The words came out of Eve easily when her younger sister gave her a concerned look. "But Alice, if Crow or I were actually imprisoned, would you really do nothing? Even if they arrested us on false charges, would you not stand up against them?"

"Huh! I—I…"

"I couldn't let that happen. I don't want to lose any family. I'm the oldest here. It's my duty to protect you and Crow."

Eve, for the first time, had cast away her contrarian outer shell and revealed her true feelings.

"If you or Crow were arrested, I'd go in alone and launch an attack. I don't care who it'd be against. The military police, the Imperial assembly, I'd punch the top person there…well, I'm half joking, though. Of course it'd be better if that never happened."

"Th-that's right, Eve!" Alicerose nodded earnestly. "We're all just on edge right now. Let's wait it out. They're calling us witches, but there's nothing to be scared of. They'll realize that sometime. We'll go back to when we all got along. That's what I believe!"

"You're so trusting, Alice… You're optimistic."

"I-is that so wrong?!"

"I never said it wasn't. You're actually mature, unlike me," Eve suddenly smiled bitterly. "I hope it ends like that…"

That small hope would be mercilessly crushed in just four days.

*   *   *

Musha was arrested for being a witch.

She'd used her astral power to commit arson and harmed normal people. The military police who came to the scene of the crime were terribly wounded.

"There's no way!"

Crossweil had come home from the grocery store, while trying to avoid prying eyes.

When Alicerose, with an expression he'd never seen before, had told Crossweil, he was at a loss for words.

"I can't believe that Musha would hurt anyone. She was so scared when she came to our house. There has to be some mistake!"

"I thought that too, but there wasn't!" Alicerose's voice quivered. This was a first. He'd never seen his usually calm and kind adoptive sister panic like this.

…Actually, what about Eve?

…Why isn't she home?

Only his younger sister had been waiting for him at home. His older sister should have been there too, but she was nowhere to be found.

"I think Eve must have left to save Musha!"

"Damn it. I've got a bad feeling about this!" He grabbed his sister's shoulders and nodded slightly. "You wait at home, Alice. I'll bring Eve back. Don't open the door for anyone!"

He turned his back to his sister and ran out the door.

He needed to stop her. He had a feeling this wasn't going to end well. In his head, it felt as though a foreboding chill seemed to be closing in on him.

…Alice is worried for Eve.

...But that's not the problem. The military police are in the most danger!

Only he knew about the many flashes of light that Eve had released while she wasn't herself. If she used that power on the police, they would all likely perish.

Eve's astral crest was larger than anyone else's, and to Crossweil this was proof that the power she possessed was stronger than the rest.

"Eve, where did you go?!"

He ran down the main road. The nearby police station had no clues for him. He ran around the spot where Musha had been arrested, but saw no sign of Eve.

"Was Musha not taken to a police station, then?"

She'd been arrested.

That was why he'd went there, but if Musha was being brought in as a witch, the people who would question her would be those who had been pressing for the astral energy plan in the first place.

"So she's at the Imperial assembly?!"

"If you or Crow were arrested, I'd go in alone and launch an attack."

Musha's arrest wasn't just a problem concerning her.

The only ones who would listen about the disparagement of witches and sorcerers were those in the highest body in the Empire. Thinking of it that way, he might find his sister at the Imperial assembly.

"But that's reckless, Eve!"

He broke into a run again, still out of breath.

His heart was thumping in his chest louder and louder. The

worst thing that could happen was if Eve went on a rampage in the Imperial assembly and injure its highest members.

By the vast silver-barred gate to the premises of the Imperial assembly...

"Please, let me see Musha!"

A tan girl was shouting, her throat raspy as armed guards surrounded her.

She didn't stop, even as they grabbed her shoulders.

"She's still only fourteen! A fourteen-year-old kid hurting people? There's no way! Someone had to have framed her!"

However...

None of the muscular guards who looked down on Eve responded. Their eyes were emotionless. Was this how they would look at a small girl?

Even after seeing her appeal to him, their gazes were distant. A chill ran down her spine as she realized they saw her with the same hollow eyes as someone observing a pebble by the roadside.

"..."

"Hey! You guys...," one of the guards said.

They weren't looking at Eve's face, but instead at her back. They were staring at the gigantic astral mark that showed through the thin shirt she wore.

"It's a witch. Yeah, that's right. We caught it smack-dab in front of the assembly gate. Tell the Eight Great Elders."

"Guh."

The look in Eve's eyes changed as she heard the guards murmur.

Instead of being treated as a girl who had come to save another innocent child arrested for a crime she didn't commit, she was being treated as a violent witch trying to free a ferocious comrade. Those were the eyes with which the guards looked at her.

"...I see. Am I—is my mark that unpleasant to you? Is that the only reason why you captured Musha, too? So she didn't actually hurt anyone. You just arrested her to make it seem justified. You just wanted to create a villain."

The guards didn't react.

They simply pulled up Eve's wrists and matter-of-factly clasped shackles on her. Crossweil cut in, trying to stop them. But right as he did that...

Sera......So Sez lu teo fel nalis pah pheno lef xel—I will purify this planet, as one of its children.

There was an explosion.

Or so it seemed to Crossweil.

The light was strong enough to burn his retinas. There was a sound loud enough to make him almost lose consciousness. The shock wave, which seemed to contort the atmosphere itself blasted at them. At the epicenter was Eve.

By the time he came to his senses, there were spider cracks in the concrete, and the bars of the gate were bent beyond recognition. Even the cars in the surrounding area had been overturned.

"Don't touch me."

The girl glowered at the guards on the ground.

The back of her shirt had been ripped apart, exposing her dark astral crest. Her flowing straw-colored hair fluttered even though there was no wind as though it had its own will.

Crossweil didn't know how to begin describing the way she carried herself. She'd awakened. She had turned into something beyond human. That was all he could think.

"…Eve?"

"Is that you, Crow?"

She turned around.

It seemed she'd only just realized he was there.

"Go home," she said.

"What are you planning on doing, Eve?! And what happened here…?"

"I'm going to release Musha." Eve turned toward the Imperial assembly that towered up ahead. "I don't need the Empire anymore. It's not where I belong."

"…What?" Realization came rushing to him at once. Eve planned to go on a rampage. She was planning to destroy the Empire, wiping out anyone who got in her way, until Musha was returned to her.

"Wait, Eve. We don't even know if Musha is here! If you destroy things randomly, it'll be a disas—"

"She's under the assembly. I feel Musha's astral power there."

"…"

He felt something cold running down his cheek. Eve was no longer the older sister he knew.

…She's the same as Yunmelngen.

…She doesn't look different, but she's acting like another person.

Eve raised a hand.

She looked at the sky as though summoning something.

"Crow, go back home," she said.

"Wait, Eve!"

She disappeared. Eve had calmly disappeared into a black void-like gate.

Just thirty minutes later, the Imperial assembly was partially destroyed by an explosion from underground.

6

A few days passed.

"It's been a while, Crow."

After being released from a long interrogation that lasted hours from the military police, Crossweil walked home and talked to Yunmelngen for the first time in a while.

"I'm myself again after ten days. Though I'm not sure if it's my human self or astral power self talking."

"…There were some really bad things happening here while you were sleeping."

"Seems like your older sister made a mess of things."

They hadn't been able to stop her. He'd more or less known. Like Yunmelngen's, the influence her astral power had on her was too strong. Then that overwhelming astral power had become enraged and blown away part of the Empire.

"How much do you know?"

"More than you would. At least about the gravity of the crime your family member committed."

They both paused for a while.

"She came into the assembly hall to take back Musha, a witch. Then she gravely injured the guards who came to meet her and destroyed the lower level of the assembly hall without leaving a trace. The Eight Great Elders were also severely wounded while they were interrogating Musha."

"Right."

"The whole event was caught on the security cameras and has been made public to the rest of the world."

This was the decisive moment, when they'd encountered a

violent witch. This hadn't been made up by the Imperial leaders. It was real.

"It looks like we've created a crystal-clear case of someone possessed by astral power who is dangerous, right in front of the whole world. It's not just Eve. This event has warranted even worse treatment toward all astral power contaminators."

"And Eve is a wanted criminal now."

"Yeah. I can't help her in this case. I'd like to ask her what happened directly, but she's not with you, is she, Crow?"

"She's not. She disappeared."

After releasing Musha, they'd both disappeared.

"I can't stop it either anymore." The Crown Prince sighed. "The Lord still isn't awake, and the Eight Great Elders have taken over the government in his place. They've been gravely injured. I'm sure you can connect the dots."

"She's made powerful people in the Empire into her enemies."

"It'll be the start of a witch hunt. Soon, persecution of astral power contaminators within the Empire will begin. Oh, that's not true. Since contaminators are viewed as the wrongdoers, they won't call it prosecution, but justice instead."

"Then what are we supposed to do?!"

"..."

Silence fell over them. It was the longest stretch of silence between them since they had started talking with each other.

"I'll be direct. This country is no longer a place for astral power contaminators, including you, Crow."

"You can't mean..."

His throat felt dry, and it took all he had to get his voice to come out.

He didn't even need to guess at what Yunmelngen was imply-
ing because it was so obvious. It was too cruel.

...We'll all be treated as criminals in the Empire.

...But we still live here.

Only the humans in the Empire called them contaminators,
witches, and sorcerers.

There was still time. They could find a country in this vast
world that might still accept them.

"Are you saying I should escape from the Empire?"

**"I have my position as the Crown Prince here. I can't pub-
licly help, but I also won't stop you. I can look the other way."**

But where would they run to? They would need to move out
of the Empire. Trying to find the thousands of people around
would be an unprecedented challenge and preparations would take
months. And where would they run? How would they live?

**"You should think about it. If it comes down to it, you can
just run with your family."**

"This is really the last resort we have..."

He'd started to feel an attachment to their home. He'd finally
gotten used to living in the Empire, too.

"I'll talk to Alice. But Eve's not around, so we don't have any
way to decide."

He hung up and started walking down the main road. Most of
the houses were dark, their lights off. He shrunk against the freez-
ing wind as he navigated using the unreliable streetlights. When
he finally arrived home, he found his sister nervously standing in
front of it.

"Crow! Oh, good. You're safe," she said.

"They were interrogating me again today. Trying to get me to
cough up Eve's location."

He wanted to know where she was, too. He had no idea what she was doing or where she was since she'd disappeared in front of the assembly.

"It must have been cold. Let's get inside."

Once they were inside, they were back in their warm and bright living room, out of the suffocating cold outside. But then everything went dark.

Had the electricity gone out? He'd thought that for a moment upon seeing the room blacked out.

Then a girl with golden hair leapt out from a black void.

"Eve?!" Crossweil said.

"Eve?! Wh-what...?!" Alicerose blinked several times at her sister.

Now that Crossweil thought of it, this was Alicerose's first time seeing her sister's power. And her power wasn't manipulating flames or wind like some magic trick. Instead, it was some godlike ability that allowed her to warp space itself.

"Eve...?"

And her sister looked entirely different as well.

Though there was no wind to speak of, Eve's golden hair continuously undulated. She also wore a cloak that seemed as though it'd been made from the shirt she'd once worn.

"Alice, Crow," she said. Her voice was emotionless as she addressed them. It was enough to make Crossweil shudder. It was almost as though it were lifeless.

"We have something to discuss," she said.

"Eep?!"

"What?!"

They hadn't even had time to blink.

As Eve grabbed their hands, the world in front of them began to fissure. He and Alicerose were both being pulled into one of the pitch-black voids.

By the time he realized what had happened, he was inside a dark abyss, as though a black curtain had been pulled down on him.

It was the inside of a black tent. In the square space around him that spread dozens of meters out all around, he saw black towers in the corners. They had the glossy finish of obsidian. Where was he? What was this place? They weren't outside or in their home. It was as though they were in some empty subspace.

"Alice!"

"Musha?!" Alicerose shouted in surprise as she caught a girl in her arms.

It was Musha. Since Eve's attack on the assembly, she had disappeared with Eve.

"You were safe, Musha?! I heard you were arrested by the military police…"

"It's all a lie! They forced me into a car and told me I was being investigated. When I tried to fight back, they blew it out of proportion and said I was being violent!"

"It was the same for me." Next, Drake, their leader from the excavation site spoke up. "The military police came to my home, too. Eve saved me before they could take me in, and brought me to this odd shelter. The same applies for everyone else here."

Crossweil then noticed that it wasn't just Musha and Drake with them. Hundreds of people, old and young, men and women were there. He saw people from the excavation site as well as those he'd seen on the streets of the Empire.

That was when he realized.

Many of the people gathered had concealed their foreheads and wrists with bandages. He didn't even need to guess what was under those.

...They're all astral power contaminators who were arrested.

...Eve has been saving all of them on her own.

She had disappeared for days.

As the Empire went into emergency alert, Eve had been taking people to this space one at a time.

"We don't need the Empire anymore." Her harsh voice rang out. "We're leaving it."

Murmurs ran through the space. Over a hundred people searched their neighbors' faces, but Crossweil alone balled his hands into fists. He'd heard this before.

...What kind of irony is this?

...We're fleeing the Empire. She's agreeing with Yunmelngen.

And was claiming that was their only option.

The Crown Prince and the girl rebelling against the Empire had both reached the same conclusion.

"Tell your family and kindred this," she said. "Take all that you have and run. If the military police obstruct you, I will eliminate them."

Her declaration of rebellion was chillingly calm. She spoke as though the police were nothing but insects.

"B-but...!" a man, unable to keep quiet, shouted. "If we turn against them, then the Imperial forces will be next!"

"I'll do the same with the Imperial forces. I'll get rid of them on my own."

"......What?!"

"I will show no mercy to anyone who stands in our way. No matter how many there are."

Silence filled the place. When faced with how much Eve had changed, and the transcendental power and self-confidence she had, everyone subconsciously realized something.

She wasn't lying.

The astral power in this small girl was strong enough to wipe out the entire Empire.

"We will carry this out in three weeks' time," she continued. "We should abandon this country as soon as we can."

"Wait, Eve!" Alicerose's strained shout echoed throughout the black space. "We're all shaken up. I don't think it'll be as easy as you think to flee from the Empire. We've all grown to love this place from living here. We can't cut ourselves off from our livelihoods, families, and friends that easily..."

"However—"

"We need more time!" Alicerose interrupted Eve.

This was the first time Crossweil had seen this happen. The younger twin was showing a resolve strong enough to interrupt her own older sister.

"Please, Eve. Please give everyone time to think."

"..."

"We need time to prepare, too. The military police are on high alert all over the Empire. They'll notice if thousands of people leave the capital. Right?"

Eve was silent. She listened seriously to her sister's pleas.

"Let's take some time to figure things out. We need to think about where we will head once we leave the Empire, how we will make a living there, and how to make sure everyone feels safe."

"..."

"Please, Eve."

There was an exceedingly long stretch of silence after that.

The two sisters stared at each other unblinkingly until the elder sister finally replied, "Okay."

Heh, Eve's expression softened for just a moment.

"Since you're smart, Alice, we'll do that. I'm no good as an older sister, after all."

After all this time, Crossweil had forgotten what his sister's smile looked like.

But that had been...

...the last time he saw it.

MEMORY ILLUMINATION 4

Plan to Flee the Empire

Half a year had passed.

The term *astral power contaminator* had all but disappeared from the Empire's vocabulary on TV and in newspapers, and even on the streets. Now they only used the words *witch* and *sorcerer*. Those possessed by astral powers would hide their crests voluntarily with bandages and had learned to avoid crowded areas.

That included him, too.

"Crossweil Gate Nebulis, is it?"

"…"

He had been stopped under a streetlight. It was nine at night, when few people were outside. He'd just finished buying groceries at an old store in an alleyway, avoiding the supermarket on the main road. Imperial soldiers waited for him, as though to block Crossweil from his destination.

Not the police, but *soldiers*.

As violent encounters with witches and sorcerers had grown,

the Imperial assembly had responded in kind by suppressing them using the Imperial forces.

"Four witches caught by the Imperial forces escaped. Just more of the Grand Witch Nebulis's destruction."

"I don't know anything about it..."

"She's your adoptive sister Eve. You lived with her half a year ago."

"That was a long time ago. Alice and I don't know where she is or what she's doing. You already tore apart our home four days earlier and didn't find anything."

"..."

The two soldiers went silent. Crossweil gave them a small nod and passed by them.

He was used to this. The interrogators on the street had simply shifted from military police to Imperial forces. His role was to calmly answer any of their questions. If he got worked up, they would use that as a pretext to arrest him. Such was life in the Empire now.

...That's why everyone puts up with it. We're almost there.

...Four days until we leave the Empire.

He balled his fists as he continued walking down the dark road to his house.

"I'm home," he called out.

"Crow, welcome back!" Alicerose was waiting for him. She was wearing an apron and preparing dinner. She had tied her silky, golden hair tied back, which made her seem all the more charming.

In the past half year, Alicerose had turned sixteen and started looking even more beautiful and mature.

It wasn't just her outward appearance that had matured. She was a calming presence that could stop conflicts better than anyone. She was the least witchlike person there could be, despite the Imperial forces' derision.

"Eve just got back too," she told him.

"What? Oh, she really has..."

Eve was lying on the floor. He hadn't noticed because of how quiet she was. She was fast asleep. Though the Imperial leaders called her the "Grand Witch" and designated her as the most dangerous of all on their hit list, she looked defenseless in her sleep.

"Some soldiers just stopped me. They wanted to know if I've seen Eve. And where she's hiding."

The Imperial forces likely wouldn't even be able to imagine that Eve lived in a subspace.

Though she mostly hid in the same black curtain that Crossweil had entered once before, she would return to their home on occasion.

...It's like a secret base.

...She uses that space to come and go so she can rescue people who have been arrested on the charge of being a witch.

Eve had saved hundreds already. All of them had fled to the subspace and were preparing for their escape from the Empire.

"Everyone's grateful for being saved by Eve. And they say that we should be able to leave the Empire without worries with her here." Alicerose lovingly stroked her sleeping older sister's hair.

They looked as though their positions should have been switched. She seemed like the older sibling lovingly taking care of her younger sister. Alicerose had always looked more mature, and the gap had only widened in the past six months.

...Eve looks like she hasn't changed.

...It's almost like time has stopped for her.

Despite Alicerose's growth, Eve hadn't grown by even a millimeter. She also had started eating considerably less.

"You can tell by looking at me. She's already almost half astral power."

*   *   *

It was two days until their escape.

When Crossweil had his first call in two weeks with Yunmelngen, the prince sounded nonchalant, as if telling him that should have been obvious after seeing her for the past six months.

"According to the Imperial forces' database, there are 7,981 people believed to be witches and sorcerers. The number has increased tenfold because the Planet's Navel is still releasing astral powers even now. Until we close the hole, there will likely be more."

"And the Empire is leaving it open while knowing that?"

"There were talks about who would do it. If anyone approaches the hole, they might also turn into a witch. We can't just carelessly go near it."

"I guess you have a point…"

"Put another way, there are many astral powers escaping from deep within the planet. And the people who've been possessed by the strongest are—"

"You and Eve."

"Yes, and that's why Eve doesn't eat. I haven't had a sip of water, either."

Astral powers had no lifespan. That was something Yunmelngen had intuited instinctively after fusing with his.

"Eve and I will likely live for many more years. Maybe a hundred, maybe a thousand. Or perhaps we'll simply disappear suddenly in a few years…"

"…You talk about it like that it doesn't involve you."

"This isn't entirely unrelated to you either, Crow."

That hit him hard. He felt as if a thorn had stabbed him right through the chest without warning.

"…Me?"

"The more compatible someone is with astral power, the more their body becomes astral power, the slower they age. Haven't you noticed? You're quite fused with it yourself."

"..."

Unintentionally, he touched the astral crest on his neck.

"Not very perceptive about yourself, are you, Crow? Well, maybe it was difficult for you to notice because Eve and I are such extreme examples."

It hadn't even so much as occurred to him. That there was a possibility his lifespan would extend considerably due to the astral power. Or that it even might be diminished.

"Oh, but also there's that."

Despite Crossweil's silence, Yunmelngen's tone hadn't changed in the slightest.

"The day after tomorrow is the birthday. Are you ready for it?"

"We're ready whenever. Even tomorrow would work."

The *birthday* was a metaphor. It was a code word used among those who knew about the escape plan.

"I've been so lonely here without any news from you lately, Crow."

"You're generally the one who's supposed to call me."

"How forlorn I am. If you go to the birthday the day after tomorrow, we won't ever see each other again."

"Huh?!"

He didn't know what to say.

Yunmelngen's usual cheerful tone had disappeared, and the prince seemed genuinely saddened. Yunmelngen wasn't participating in the escape plan because he was the Crown Prince. Almost all the astral power contaminators would be gone in three days. However, only Yunmelngen, the most conspicuous one, would be staying in the Empire.

*   *   *

"More astral power contaminators will be born after this. And all over the world."

"If even I leave, then who will stop the persecution within the Empire?"

They needed someone on the inside who could correct the prejudices against witches.

Yunmelngen had decided only he could do that.

"You're not the type to change your mind even if I asked you to come now."

"I'll be sad not being able to see you anymore, though."

Ah-ha-ha, he heard a laugh over the line. It was the weakest chuckle he'd heard from Yunmelngen yet.

"I'll be enthroned in the place of my father, as he's still in a coma. Even in this state, if I become the Lord, I'll have a lot more power."

"Are you going to be okay?"

"I'll have someone else go in place of me for public appearances."

"You said something about the Eight Great Elders. How's your fight with them going?"

"We still disagree plenty. But who cares about them? If I can become Lord, I should be able to do something."

"......I see."

They would flee the Empire. The contaminators needed to escape persecution first. But the fear and hatred of witches would still remain rooted in the entire Empire.

...That needs to be settled later.

...In other words, we're leaving all the work to Yunmelngen.

Was that really the right thing to do?

That's what he'd been thinking about the past six months. Or rather, he'd used thinking about it as a way of putting it off until now.

"Crow, promise me one thing."

"What's that?"

"Once I become Lord, if I'm able to stop all persecution of witches...when that time comes, come by and visit, will you?"

"..."

"If you can promise that, I'll really be able to give my all."

"Invite me whenever you want," Crossweil didn't hesitate to reply. Compared to Yunmelngen's resolve to stay alone in the Empire, the prince's request was modest and easy to make good on.

"I'll be sure to come back to the Empire. Even if it's years or decades from now."

"......Okay." Yunmelngen's reply was still slightly lacking. **"See you, Crow. Hope you fare well outside the Empire."**

"You too."

The Imperial assembly.

Due to the destruction caused by the Grand Witch Nebulis, half of the building had been destroyed, and was constantly on the verge of collapsing.

In the rubble of an underground room...

"An attempt at enacting an escape."

"Watching the last criminal apprehended as the curtain falls will be most beautiful."

The light of eight hazy monitors...

There, eight men and women, young and old, were displayed.

"An escape plan that the witches and sorcerers have come up with. This is no great getaway. It is an act of rebellion against the

capital disguised in the discord that will come with an escape. And we may assume that it could possibly be an attack on His Excellency and the Crown Prince."

"Isn't that right, Drake?"

"Raise your face, Drake In Empire."

"..."

The radiance of the spotlights poured down on Drake from overhead.

Under the large monitors that displayed right humanoid figures, the young man bit his lip. It was almost as though he were a courtroom witness. He looked deeply worried.

"You are a felon."

"After all, you planned to burn the Imperial capital to the ground following the Grand Witch Nebulis's plan three days from now."

"No! We're just leaving the—"

"You simply need to make the testimony. That is all."

"Huh!" The boy's eyes opened wide.

He had been taken to the Eight Great Elders, the staff officers to the Lord, without a clue on what and how they would question him.

"A deal. Instead of throwing you into prison, we will allow you to live your days peacefully in the Empire. That will apply to both you and your family. In exchange, you need only testify for us."

"That the Grand Witch Nebulis's true aim is to take over the Empire."

"With the power she has, would it not be easy for her to turn the capital into a sea of flames?"

"You don't want me to confess about the escape plan, then?"

He had been too naive. The supreme authorities of the Empire sought not a confession but a false testimony to an even greater crime.

"But what will you get by having me do that...?"

The elders did not answer. The long silence as good as told him he did not need to know.

"Think it over, Drake. Where will you go once you leave the Empire?"

"Witches and sorcerers are feared all over the world. Even if you leave, no country will accept you. You will wander borders, suffering from the cold and hunger."

"......Uh. I..."

They coaxed him, directly aiming for his weaknesses. The elders knew this, and that it was the truth.

"It's the Grand Witch Nebulis's fault, not yours."

"And the same applies for Musha. We planned to put her under our protection. But the Grand Witch attacked our assembly hall and maimed dozens of innocents."

"You cannot stay in the Empire only because of the Grand Witch Nebulis's actions."

"You have no reason to sympathize with her. You should break ties with her."

The floor tile split with a loud clanking sound. A portable recording device rose from the floor.

"The Empire is your homeland."

"You are only being ousted from it because of the Grand Witch. Don't you detest her?"

"...Ngh."

Those were like a devil's whispers to him. Though he knew better, his arm reached for the device in front of his eyes.

"Now, let us hear of it, Drake."

"Tell us your testimony to get revenge on the Grand Witch Nebulis, the reason you cannot stay in the Empire."

MEMORY ILLUMINATION 5

That Which Renders the World to Pieces

1

The birthday.

Thousands of witches and sorcerers would be leaving at daybreak.

"_____"

Yunmelngen was lying on his bed watching the sunrise, not having slept at all.

"Crow..."

He held the comm that was next to the bed. He wanted to call his friend. He tried to think of something, anything to speak to Crossweil about. He just wanted to hear his friend's voice.

But it was no use.

Crossweil was already on the first train out with the others.

That train led to the border. If he could simply reach it

and provide identification, leaving the Empire would be easy. That even applied to witches and sorcerers possessed by astral power.

"There's no law that forbids astral power contaminators from leaving. As long as they don't get in a dispute with the border soldiers. I hope things go without incident for you, Crow."

It was vexing. Why was Yunmelngen awake now of all times? He wished that he were unconscious like he had been just a few days ago. He had spent the past few hours in agony, helplessly worrying about Crow.

"Ahh…I know this isn't like me. A Crown Prince shouldn't be so infatuated with a commoner."

He tossed the comm to the corner of the bed. It was heavy to carry. He tried to rest in bed, even if it was impossible and buried his face into a pillow.

"…?"

Yunmelngen's inhuman hearing caught an odd sound.

It was the footsteps of many people running. They weren't simply in a hurry. The footfalls were stifled as though the people were sneaking closer. They stopped in front of Yunmelngen's room.

"Crown Prince, Your Highness." He didn't recognize the voice. "We have arrived for your physical exam today. May I open the door?"

He had a bad feeling about this. His silver fur stood on end, and he felt a chill he'd never experienced before. So he answered, **"No."**

"Why not?"

"I do not feel well today. I cannot get out of bed, so the exam will have to wait until tomorrow."

"Then all the more reason to have it now. Won't you please open the door?"

"Who are you all?"

It wasn't just one person but several. He could implicitly sense the many people waiting in front of the door, attempting to hide.

"I'll say it again. I do not feel well. You should also know that I haven't been stable since what happened to me. If you must, then—?!"

The door burst open. The thick mechanical door was blown away.

"A bomb?!"

Why? He didn't even have the time to question the situation as he leapt up from the bed. In the fumes and smoke, several human silhouettes dashed into the room. They were an armed group wearing goggles to hide their identities. They weren't the Imperial soldiers, nor the guards. Who were they, then?

"Where did you mercenaries come from?!"

"..."

All of them pointed their guns, large enough to be able to take down a bear, at him wordlessly. They were too close in range for Yunmelngen to avoid.

"Farewell."

Vivid purple blood splattered in the Crown Prince's chambers.

2

Morning, five o'clock.

Along the skyline, between the gaps in the buildings, the faint sun began to rise. While most of the citizens were still in bed…

…a crimson explosion shook the quiet capital.

The asphalt roads were blown to smithereens and flew away. Buildings with broken glass swayed from the force of the impact and fell over each other like dominos.

"Ah?!"

"Uh?! What was that huge explosion…?"

Alicerose screamed at the thunderous roar. Next to her, Crossweil turned around to look at the disastrous scene.

"Is it a fire?"

Dense fog wafted up in the horizon, as well as embers that dyed the sky bright red. They were at the Eleventh Avenue Terminal. Almost a thousand people from the "first unit" had been boarding the first train heading to the border when the explosion happened.

"Is that at Castle Tower Seat?"

That was where Yunmelngen lived. But there was no way such a thing would have occurred there. It was the Empire's most important building.

"Move, Crow."

"What?"

Eve looked up silently at the sky and raised both her hands.

I call upon the outer layer of the planet.

The protection of the atmosphere.

He wasn't sure whether it was the wind or just air, but some sort of invisible shield had spread, covering the terminal they had gathered in. He could feel it on his skin.

The first train in the terminal was also swallowed up by a raging fire.

The blast fell on them like an avalanche. Shock waves strong enough to form holes in the concrete walls rippled out in all directions. Before the steel could be scorched and the heat wave could reach them, the atmospheric shield stopped it.

"The train exploded?!"

They had barely made it. Had Eve not protected them, everyone near the train would have been blown away by the explosion.

...Based on the timing and location, it couldn't have been a coincidence.

...They were trying to purge us as we were boarding the train!

He didn't know who wished them dead.

The one thing they did know for certain was that someone had leaked their plan to escape. And the person who found out must have held ill will toward astral power contaminators.

"Wh-what's going on here?!" Musha was pale. "Th-that bomb was meant for us, wasn't it?! Why?!"

They were only trying to leave the Empire.

They hadn't been trying to create any problems for anyone, yet someone had tried to stop them in this way.

"Level one emergency."

"All wards between First to Eleventh Avenue are ordered to evacuate."

*   *   *

A warning had been issued.

It wasn't simply coming from the Terminal, but also from the streets.

"Twelve locations, including Castle Tower Seat, have been bombed. The fire is spreading. Evacuate immediately."

"The culprits are believed to be the Grand Witch Nebulis and her followers."

…What?

Crossweil couldn't believe his ears.

While he understood the words, he couldn't grasp the meaning of them.

…The Grand Witch Nebulis? Isn't that Eve?

…But she's been by my side this whole time!

It must have been a misunderstanding or a false accusation. She was a hero who had saved hundreds of people from the bomb on the first train.

"Wh-what's going on…Eve?!" Alicerose looked at her sister. As everyone stared at her, she looked up at the sky.

"I see." Her voice was stifled and almost made them shudder. "So they will go that far to make me out to be a witch."

There was another explosion. The flames shooting up from below and embers floating above were quickly turning the Imperial skies a dark red.

…The capital is burning.

…But we didn't do this. Someone's trying to pin this on us!

Their plan had been exposed.

That was when they had failed. Their escape from the capital had been changed into an uprising.

*   *   *

"The Grand Witch Nebulis has been spotted at Eleventh Avenue Terminal."

"Those in the vicinity should stay indoors. All other citizens should take shelter as soon as possible."

"This is no joke!" a middle-aged man wearing a backpack yelled. After his family had turned into astral power contaminators, even though he hadn't, he'd decided to escape the capital with them. "We haven't done anything! This explosion was—"

A bullet flew. As though to tear through his pleas, the sound of the opened fire rang out immediately after.

"Surrender."

From within the flames that licked at the building, armored cars came into view. Lines of gun-toting infantry also appeared. Crossweil could hear an even larger tank coming from behind the lines.

"We have a message for the Grand Witch Nebulis's sect."

"We have come to arrest you for the attack on Castle Tower Seat and arson, as well as on charges of destroying the capital. You have nowhere to run."

"Surrender."

What would they do after conceding? Because they hadn't resisted, hundreds of their own had already been imprisoned. They had learned down to their bones that surrender meant nothing in the past half year. Then what were they to do?

They could only run.

Everyone subconsciously knew that.

The train was destroyed, so they had to run on their own two legs. First, they needed to leave the Empire. But they were surrounded by raging flames closing in on them from all sides.

"Ruuun!"

"Scatter! Get out of the capital. Aim for the border!"

Dozens of voices yelled all at once. Over a thousand people fled in all directions from the burning front of the Terminal.

"Crow!"

"Over here, Alice! We need to run, too!"

He started to sprint with Alicerose.

...*Who set the capital on fire?!*

...*And the Lord's residence. What if something had happened to Yunmelngen...?*

But first he needed to focus on himself. If they couldn't run from this place, they would be caught and thrown in prison.

"Crow! In front!" Alicerose pointed ahead at the main road.

"They've surrounded us?!"

Imperial soldiers were running out one after another from the side alleys with guns in hand. Tanks and armored vehicles were approaching them from behind. They were being closed in on from both the front and back.

"Stop!" Someone shouted a warning from the armored vehicle. "The Eleventh Avenue Terminal is surrounded. We are arresting you on suspicion of bombing Castle Tower Seat and setting fire to seventeen locations within the Imperial capital."

"This can't be real! We haven't done anything!" Crossweil yelled back, spreading his arms out.

However, the pleas didn't reach them, which he already knew would happen. That was because they had been basically caught red-handed. To the Imperial soldiers, at least, over a thousand astral power contaminators had gathered in front of the Terminal—that was all they saw.

They were the rebellion led by the witch who had set fire to the capital.

"This is your final warning! Halt."

"If you resist or run, we will fire."

Then someone answered that threat.

"Alice, Crow, get down."

Flames rose. They were not the crimson ones that burned the capital. The wall of flames that seemed to envelop the tanks and armored vehicles were a bright violet.

"Urk?!"

As they were faced with these unknown flames, the vehicles stopped one after another.

"I'll handle the soldiers. They're likely after me more than anyone else."

Eve stepped forward.

"You get out of the capital first."

"Eve?!" Alicerose cried. "You can't. You can't do something so dangerous. You need to come with us!"

"Alice." She turned around. Her astral crest, bigger than anyone's, was apparent on her back. "I'm the older sister. Don't worry about me."

"Huh!"

"Come on, go. Crow, you protect Alice."

That stirred something in him.

It wasn't her words, but the way she seemed to carry the weight of being an older sister around her.

"Alice, we're running!" Crossweil yelled.

He grabbed her hand before she could protest and broke out into a run.

The sky was dyed red.

To escape from the capital, which was being engulfed in flames, Crossweil chose alleyways instead of the main roads. Among the many narrow and complicated passages, there was one route that led to the outskirts of the capital. This was a path even the locals did not know about.

"Crow, everyone else is…"

"Everyone's using their own path to escape. We need to run too, or we'll get caught up in the fires!"

The flames enveloping the capital were spreading.

It leapt from building to building and onto private homes. There were people fleeing from their own homes with only the clothes on their backs.

…*It's not just astral power contaminators.*

…*The fire's so big, everyone living in the capital has to escape.*

They ran with the fires pursuing them.

"Alice, all we're thinking about is running right now. If we get caught, we wouldn't be able to face Eve again—ah?!"

He stopped in his tracks in the narrow passage. In front of him was a wall. Iron plates and planks of wood towered over them like a mountain blocking their path.

"They saw through it!"

This was what the Imperial forces meant by "surrounded," then.

Their escape plan had been leaked. They must have closed off all routes the day before or the day before that.

"Crow, behind us!" Alicerose's face crumpled as she heard combat boots approaching from behind them.

They had nowhere to go. Armed soldiers were behind them. Scrap wood had been piled in front of their eyes, obstructing their escape.

…*What do I do?! It'd be impossible to force our way through their forces.*

…*Can we climb the barricade? No, they would attack while we're going up.*

Reality was beyond cruel. Eve was out there stopping all those soldiers on her own, meanwhile, he couldn't even take what remained of his precious family to safety. Not with this mountain obstructing them.

...Wait.

...I've been in a situation like this before. When his way had been blocked.

When he'd snuck into the Lord's residence.

The mechanical door had refused to move when he'd reached Yunmelngen's room. What had he done back then?

"...Alice, get behind me."

"Crow?"

"I'm going to try something reckless."

With the pile of planks and iron pipes in front of him, he touched the astral crest on his neck. He needed the same inhuman strength from when he had forced open the door of the Crown Prince's room.

For the first time, he prayed for it. For the first time, he prayed to the astral power that he had been trying to ignore until now.

...Please lend me your strength. It can even be a trade.

...If you can give me the power to get out of here, I'll accept astral power for the rest of my life!

For a moment, his crest glittered. It was as though it was responding to his determination...or his offer.

"Mooooove!"

He ran at the wall, throwing all he had into ramming into it. The moment Crossweil tackled the towering pile that had to weigh hundreds of kilograms, sending pieces of it flying. It was as though he were a train running right through it. The wires holding together the barricade tore to pieces and scraps of wood flew about.

"......Huh? Y-you did this, Crow...?!"

"......Haah...ah...astral power that only works through brute-force doesn't really look cool."

He ran through the path that was now filled with the wreckage.

Crossweil worried for his other friends, who had scattered in all directions. They were all likely using any paths they could remember and any means they could come up with to also escape.

We got through the barricade.

...That only worked because I happened to have the right astral power possessing me.

There were more people than not who didn't have that. Among the names in the witch list that the authorities of the Empire had revealed, there were many who simply had been possessed by astral power but didn't have an ability.

That was the case for Alicerose. Because they were the same as ordinary civilians, they needed help from people like him and Eve.

"The barrier has been destroyed. It's a higher-rank witch. You have permission to open fire."

"We're picking up astral energy readings! To the right!"

He could hear the loud orders being barked in the narrow alleyway behind them.

"Crow, they're getting closer!"

"Run, Alice!"

He took Alicerose's hand and turned right at the crossroad.

However, instead of losing the soldiers, the faster they ran, the closer the soldiers seemed. He felt something cold running down his neck as he made that realization. Their search was frighteningly accurate.

... The alleys we're heading into are supposed to be like a maze.

...How do the soldiers know where we are?

Astral energy readings. He'd heard the unfamiliar term multiple times from behind him.

"They couldn't possibly be...?!"

He touched the astral crest on his neck.

He realized the frightful truth. Had the Empire already created a device that detected astral power's energy?

"Alice, we can't use the alleys. There's no point in even hiding!"

"What?!"

"They've got something like a heat sensor. They can detect astral energy. If they can find us in the alleyways, it'll be faster to cross through the main roads!"

They'd use the fastest, most direct way out of the capital. As soon as Crossweil headed out onto the main road, in an instant, he knew that decision was a mistake. He saw something he shouldn't have.

The witches being taken by the Imperial forces.

Some had been shot and were still bleeding, while others were crying and screaming.

However, the witches were not the only victims. There were just about as many Imperial soldiers bleeding on the ground as there were witches.

It was not a one-sided fight. Both sides had been equally harmed. Eve had led several astral power contaminators who wielded powerful abilities.

And they had put that power to use. The asphalt had been broken into pieces, the tanks torn in half, and the armored cars mangled to an unrecognizable degree. There were no victors here. Soldiers and witches alike had fallen, and both sides had bled.

"What is this…?"

The scene was so gruesome that he couldn't say anything else.

How had things ended up like this? They had simply wanted to run to live in peace. The Imperial forces had come to suppress the witches and sorcerers they believed to have set fire to the capital. There was no true villain. All of them had just done what they could to survive, and none of them had done anything wrong by it.

Both sides continued to be harmed.

Among them was a girl called the Grand Witch.

"Eve!"

"Huh! Alice?!" Eve turned around, farther down on the main road.

Her face was covered in soot from the smoke and embers. Her cheek was cut, as though someone had sliced at her and blood from her forehead had run into her eye.

"Eve, your wounds…!" Alicerose went pale.

Eve had likely been grazed by bullets. She had protected herself from direct hits, but some had been unavoidable. She also had a deep wound that looked like it had come from someone gouging a knife into her.

"Stop, Eve! Let's run!" Alicerose yelled when she saw her sister's many injuries.

"After we save the others! You too, Alice! Don't come out here. Hurry and get out of the capital!"

"…"

"Alice?"

She didn't let her older sister continue. Alice shook off Cross-weil's hand as he tried to stop her and had run out of cover and straight into the middle of the road. She spread her arms in front of the Imperial soldiers and their weapons.

"Everyone, stop!"

Her lament echoed through the fiery capital. Eve and Crossweil didn't have the time to stop her as Alicerose ran to a mother and daughter crouched in the rubble. They were both astral power contaminators and were simply looking for some-where safe.

The Imperial soldiers even pointed their guns at them.

"Alice?!"

"Alice, stop!"

"Please, we haven't done anything. We didn't set this fire...!" Alicerose's eyes were red and swollen as she begged the soldiers. She was protecting the mother and daughter from their weapons. "We're just trying to leave the country! Please, listen to us. No one wants this fight. Why are—"

A shot rang out.

Amid the echoing cannon fire and the crackling embers, it was unlikely anyone had heard the shot.

Eve and Crossweil hadn't.

And before they could understand what happened—

Blood spurted from Alicerose's shoulder, and she fell back.

She didn't scream.

Alicerose's knees gave out, and she silently collapsed in front of the cowering mother and child's eyes.

"Alice?!"

Crossweil ran as fast as he could.

...*She was shot. Where? Her shoulder? Was it through her chest?!*

...*Was it only one?!*

His mind had gone blank.

But then he realized the Imperial soldiers' guns aimed for him next. He grabbed his sister as they were about to open fire.

So aves cal pile—come, staff of the heavens.

Crack.

On the other side, where space seemed to have fractured, the bullets aimed for him, his sister, and the mother and child had been swallowed up.

"I understand now..."

He heard a voice from above. The Imperial capital's skies were dark, as though rain clouds had suddenly materialized. A sinister black miasma swirled about, blocking even the sunlight.

In the center of that, the Grand Witch looked down emotionlessly upon the Imperial forces.

"This world has no heroes or saviors. If there were, why would my family have gotten hurt...? Run...you'll just be hurt..."

Dark currents of air began to coalesce. A black twisted staff appeared in Eve's right hand.

"I will destroy the Empire."

With her magic staff, she looked exactly like the witches of fairy tales.

"I am a witch, and the Imperial soldiers are enemies."

She brought down her staff. The moment Crossweil saw

that, the very air screeched. Space ruptured. Buildings blew away like they were sandcastles. The asphalt roads were stripped off the ground and turned into particles as they were blown up. Armored cars and tanks flew about likes leaves in the wind as they sailed into the sky. The destruction was not accompanied by any sound.

Before he knew it, the Imperial capital's streets had transformed into a wasteland of rubble.

"Shut up."

Using her staff, she once again mowed through them with the void.

A shock wave greater than a missile sounded out and blew five tanks—the reinforcement—across the horizon.

The road was quiet.

"…"

Eve looked down from the sky. She was likely watching the fallen soldiers, feeble and incapable as ants. The tides had turned.

Because the Grand Witch Nebulis had awakened, the Imperial forces were no longer the hunters. They had become the witches' prey.

"I should have done this from the start," Eve murmured, her eyes still hollow. "The Empire hurt my sister, so I might as well make it disappear."

She held her staff at the ready. She aimed at the Imperial soldiers who had been observing everything from the shadows of the wreckage.

"W-withdraw! Hurry!"

Dozens of soldiers threw down their guns and ran.

Eve lifted her staff a third time.

"You think I'll let you escape?"

"...Eve...stop..." Alicerose muttered from within Cross-weil's arms.

Crossweil had heard her whisper as he held his hand over her reddening shoulder.

"Stop it...I'm...fine. Stop. I don't want you to hurt anyone else...just because I got injured..."

But her voice didn't reach her sister.

The buildings crumbled with a thunderous roar. The flames crackled as they spread. There was no way Alicerose's small voice could reach her sister.

"Eve..."

"Eve, that's enough! Stop it!" Crossweil yelled in her place.

Faced with Eve's cruelty, the Imperial forces were likely chilled to the bone with fear. That the witches had set fire to the capital—a scenario that had been spread through lies—now had become reality.

...Because of the battle with Eve, the Imperial forces have almost been annihilated.

...The buildings have been destroyed, and the ground has been pulverized.

They couldn't call this a misunderstanding anymore.

Seeing this destruction, no person could say they weren't frightened of witches. That they were dangerous monsters would likely be etched into the Imperials' hearts forever.

"That's enough, sister!" Crossweil yelled. "The flames have spread, and we need to get out of here!"

"..."

She didn't act like his voice had gotten through to her, either.

And it was with great irony that it hadn't. Though Eve had gone on a rampage because of her family being injured, she was so far gone in her rage that she couldn't hear her family anymore.

"Disappear, Empire."

The witch swung her staff.

She was bringing down the staff of the heavens on the Imperial soldiers who were running away when a small figure leapt out from the shadow of a building.

"Wait."

It was someone small wearing a large raincoat.

Because of the hood drawn low over their face, Crossweil couldn't see their features, but he was the only one to draw in his breath. It was the voice he was most familiar with only after his family—his conversation partner.

"Yunmelngen?!"

"Hey, Crow. Looks like things didn't go well for either of us, did they?"

Yunmelngen removed his hood. When he did, Alicerose and the mother and child behind Crossweil screamed.

It was a beast. With giant ears on top its head, and a tail like a fox's just barely visible underneath the raincoat.

"You don't look too surprised, Eve. Well, I suppose we're similar, when it comes to being monsters."

"..."

The Grand Witch looked down on the beastperson from the sky. The two beings who possessed the greatest astral powers in the world met for the first time.

"Oh, perhaps it was bold of me to assume we're on a first-name basis. That's what Crow called you, so I did too, but I suppose Nebulis would be more appropriate."

"You..."

"Even in this state, I'm still the Crown Prince. We met at the

Planet's Navel, remember? Unfortunately, I don't, but Crow has told me an awful lot about you."

The beastperson peered at the sky. Instead of staring at Eve, he looked at the endless embers flowing about.

"The Imperial capital will eventually be burned to the ground."

"So what?"

"You weren't the one who created the fire, right?"

"And?"

Her replies were cold, nearly heartless. The flames engulfing the capital were likely the work of someone's schemes. However, Eve intended to destroy the city regardless. They had hurt the astral power contaminators and her younger sister. She knew that the Empire had done those deeds.

"I'd like to talk." Yunmelngen looked up at the Grand Witch. **"I'll let you go. I'll give out an order to remove the guards from the borders so you can leave. So if you please, don't destroy the capital more than you already have."**

"......What did you say?"

"Look, the capital has been burned down."

Under the red skies, the buildings were ablaze and being charred black. This was no longer a battle between astral power contaminators and Imperial soldiers. It was simply an unprecedented fire. If they didn't work to put out the fire immediately, things would likely end in catastrophe.

"Tens of thousands have already lost their homes. I'd like to avoid any other victims."

"You think you have the right to say that?!" she bellowed from the skies. "The Imperials! Who cares?! We faced persecution and abuse at their hands as their forces tried to provoke us!"

"Yes. And it's my fault for not stopping it…as you can see."

The raincoat went flying off. He showed his silver form as the flames continued to burn in the background.

There were bullet marks and purple blood on his fur.

Had he been a normal person, he likely would have died instantly. He had only survived because he was no longer human. It occurred to Crossweil that his injuries were bullet wounds.

…Only military police and Imperial soldiers have guns.

…Did they shoot him?!

It was proof that someone had tried to take the Crown Prince's life.

"As you can see, Nebulis, there is someone who is trying to tear apart the Empire."

Yunmelngen simply showed his bloody form to the witch in the sky.

"They were the ones who agitated the public to turn against the astral power contaminators. They deceived the Imperial assembly and the Imperial forces. I just don't have concrete proof."

"…"

"And Nebulis, I'm sure you've noticed, and that the astral power possessing your body has told you as well. There's no meaning to fighting here."

"Why?" she asked.

"The true calamity still remains at the core of the planet."

Silence fell. Crossweil and Alicerose were also quiet. They didn't know what this true calamity was.

…Yunmelngen, what are you talking about?

…You never mentioned that to me before!

"Sorry, Crow. I wanted to tell you during a less exciting time." Yunmelngen kept his back to Crossweil. **"But Nebulis, I know that you've felt it, at least. That I'm not lying. The astral powers coming to the surface were running from the planet's core."**

"…"

"I need your powers. Your enemy isn't the Empire."

"Was that all you wanted to say?" She uttered it with such venom, almost like a witch's curse.

As her voice echoed from above, Crossweil could feel the very wrath and hatred in her voice.

"The Imperials were riled up by someone, you say? That doesn't lessen the severity of their crimes! I loathe the soldiers that hurt my sister and those that degraded my friends! Yunmelngen, I don't care about this calamity you speak of!"

"So you'll simply annihilate us?"

"I will! In order to protect my friends and family!"

"Unfortunately, it seems you've transformed into a witch down to your very heart."

There was a flash from the beast. He had shown a glint of his sharp fangs from the corner of his mouth.

"In that case, I suppose I'll need to stop you to protect my country."

"You? Stop me?"

"With my power, it's not impossible, even if a wrong call is made on who the winner is."

A whirlwind began to form.

As the flames engulfing the Empire grew stronger, wind began to flow between the beast and the witch that was cold enough to freeze their sweat.

It was starting. Or rather, it had already started.

The two who had fused with their astral powers the most were about to fight, possibly to their deaths.

...Wait, they can't be serious.

...Is that really the only thing they can do?!

What good would come from fighting?! But when he thought about it, the two had also come to the same conclusions about the future. That was where the escape plan had come from. Yunmelngen, who had made the suggestion first, had recommended that to Crossweil while deciding behind the scenes to stay in the Empire. Eve had also led the plan to escape despite being scorned by others as the Grand Witch.

...The two of them did more than anyone for astral power contaminators!

...Why are they fighting each other now?!

Was there really no other alternative? His beloved sister or his genial friend? He didn't want to lose either of them. How could he stop them?

...There's no point in just telling them to stop or calm down.

...There needs to be an incentive that will make both stop.

What could he do? The only route that would prevent the two from fighting right now was...

"Wait!" As the flames approached him, Crossweil shouted as loudly as he could. "Eve, Yunmelngen! Both of you!"

However...

Neither the beast nor the witch were likely to simply agree with him.

"Sorry, Crow, this is something that I can't avoid."

"Out of the way, Crow. You need to leave the capital with Alice as fast as you can."

"..."

He stepped forward silently and stopped right in front of Yunmelngen's eyes. Then, for the first time, he turned to Eve, who was floating above him, and spread his arms. He was protecting Yunmelngen.

"Crow?!" Eve's eyes opened wide. "What are you doing?! Get out of the way. I need to wipe the person behind you off the face of the planet!"

"I thought about it..."

He addressed Eve, Alicerose, who was behind him, and Yunmelngen, who looked at him with surprise.

"I'm going to stay in the Empire."

"Uh?! Crow!" Eve's face twitched.

She couldn't understand what her little brother had told her. But this was the only conclusion he could come to in this battle where every single second mattered.

"Crow...what do you mean?!" Alice shouted.

"Sorry, Alice. You couldn't rely on me right at the most crucial moment."

He turned away from Alice's weak gaze. He couldn't stand to look at her strained face. This had been his last resort, the option he had agonized over and had been uncertain about.

"But this is the only way... It's all I can think of."

He avoided Alicerose's eyes and looked up at Eve.

"Eve, take Alice and the others and evacuate right now. You're the only one who can protect everyone after leaving the Empire."

"Crow, what are you…?!"

"I'm helping the prince out."

He turned his head to look at the silver-haired beastperson who stared back at him in adoration.

"Even if you go on a rampage in the Empire, no one's going to listen. He's the only one who can change the Empire from within. But he can't make public appearances like that, even as the Lord. Someone else needs to do it."

"**Crow…**" He could hear a sob threatening to come out in Yunmelngen's voice. The no-longer-human Crown Prince was on the verge of saying something.

Ris sia sohia, Ahz cia r-teo, So Ez xiss clar lef mihas xel—I will release it now. Listen to the song of the planet's end.

The ground beneath his feet began to tremble from the planet's core, triggered by the magic words spoken. And suddenly, Crossweil felt dizzy and a chill overwhelming him. For a moment, he thought he was going to lose consciousness.

…It's getting colder still.

…What was that voice just now?! What did I just hear?!

It hadn't been human. The moment he had heard the voice that seemed to have been issued from deep, deep within the ground, his whole body felt like it had been shackled. It wasn't just him.

"**…No, don't come near me!**"

"Yunmelngen?!"

Yunmelngen collapsed on the spot. He was panting and beads of sweat had formed on his forehead.

"**…How was that…? You understand now, Nebulis… You must have felt its words of power. You still think you need to fight the Empire?**"

"Tsk!"

The girl had fallen. She was kneeling on the ground and couldn't stand, panting in the same way as Yunmelngen.

...*It wasn't just me.*

...*Eve and Yunmelngen felt it, too.*

But it wasn't the same for everyone. The mother and child behind Alicerose were looking around as though trying to locate what had happened.

"...Silence, Yunmelngen." Eve gritted her teeth. She cursed her shaking knees as she stood up and staggered toward Alicerose. "I'll allow you to live for Crow's sake... But my hatred for the Empire has not abated in the slightest. You want to change the Empire? I'd like to see you try..."

She placed a hand on Alicerose's back.

"Let's go, Alice. You're bleeding an awful lot from your shoulder. We need to get you treated before anything else."

"W-wait, Eve! What about Crow?!"

"..." Eve was silent.

He knew it was his responsibility to answer her.

"Alice," he said, this time not avoiding her eyes. Crow gave his beloved family the best smile he could. "Thank you. This is how we're ending the half year we spent together in the Empire, but it was a lot of fun because you and Eve were around."

"...Huh!"

"Take care of the wound on your shoulder. You need to get treatment right away once you get to safety."

"Crow!"

"Please be careful," he said.

He tried to show her that she didn't need to worry about him.

He cursed his shaking legs and fought to keep watch until they left.

*　　*　　*

Then the twins disappeared.

It was Eve's power.

They were engulfed in a black whirlwind. Then his family disappeared entirely from the Empire.

"Good-bye, sisters…"

As the capital burned, Crossweil bit his lip, all alone.

MEMORY ILLUMINATION 6

A Future Where the Past Is Someday Visible

The Imperial capital Harkenweltz burned to the ground.

The bombs planted all over the Empire had ignited a fire that swallowed the buildings and people, dying the capital red. Crossweil watched the whole thing from a hill overlooking the city as he was powerless to do anything else.

"We didn't light this," he said.

"I know. I told Nebulis that, too."

Yunmelngen, who was next to him and lying on the grass, spoke curtly. The prince had said he didn't want to watch the capital burn. Instead, he had been lying down and looking up at the sky the whole time.

"I've just realized this, but fire from astral power extinguishes immediately. These flames keep going. There's someone who lit this fire to make it look like it was a witch. But there's no way it was. They'll pin this fire and everything else on Nebulis."

The Grand Witch Nebulis had destroyed the capital. It was true that she had destroyed the streets, and both the Imperial soldiers and citizens had witnessed that. She was a monster. After this, that impression of her would likely be solidified.

"Who's behind it? Assassins tried to hurt you too, right?"

"They wouldn't tell me anything. But I have a hunch."

".......Who?"

"The Eight Great Elders."

Yunmelngen let out a sigh.

"They're the only ones with enough power to do something of this scale, but it's just by process of elimination. Unfortunately, I have no proof."

Yunmelngen slowly raised himself from the grass. He placed a hand on his forehead and grabbed his own bangs.

"Crow..."

There was rage in his soft voice.

"We don't have time to wait anymore. I need to ascend to the throne immediately so I have the authority to sweep them out. I'll make sure they pay for burning down the capital."

"But you don't have evidence."

"So then we just have to find it."

Yunmelngen stood. He brushed off the leaves clinging to him.

"There are more astral powers being born in this world. Eventually, there may be one among them who can see the past. If it possesses a human—"

"You really think someone that convenient will just show up one day?"

"We'll find them. I don't care how long it takes. It'll take time to restore the capital anyway. We can take fifty years, or even a century. I know it's going to be a lot of work, though."

He let out a sigh.

The Crown Prince, soon to be Lord, squinted with happiness.

"Thank you, Crow. I'm happy you stayed."

MEMORY ILLUMINATION 7

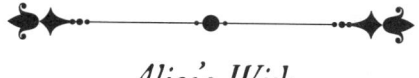

Alice's Wish

1

A decade later.

Far to the north of the Imperial lands, the astral power contaminators built a small country.

In the past ten years, they had learned to control their astral powers and dubbed themselves astral mages. The Grand Witch Nebulis led them. And so, that small country was dubbed Nebulis Sovereignty.

To Crossweil Gate Nebulis, all of those events felt as though they had happened yesterday, in the blink of an eye.

In those ten years, as the Nebulis twins developed their small country, the Empire built a new capital.

The Imperial capital Yunmelngen.

Though the city was named after its new Lord, it had not been built from scratch, but instead restored. After the Grand Witch Nebulis had turned the capital into a sea of flames from her revolt, Yunmelngen ordered the buildings to be made heat-resistant.

At a corner of an Imperial road…

"Hey, did you hear?" the Imperial soldiers were whispering to each other all over. "A new vortex turned up on the east coast. They found one in a western neutral city, too."

"There are more and more new witches every day. Even in the countries near us and within our allies."

"Think they'll move to Nebulis Sovereignty?"

"That's right. The population in the witch country keeps multiplying. At this rate, they'll turn into a huge nation."

There was a weariness to what the soldier said.

As the country that had ousted all astral power contaminators, it was only natural for them to fear the strengthening of the Nebulis Sovereignty.

"…" Passing through the gathering of soldiers, Crossweil walked silently down the main road, two swords at his side.

An adhesive to seal off his astral energy was on his neck. If that peeled off, his astral energy would be detected, and he would be ousted from the Empire.

"…"

He headed to Castle Tower Seat.

Ten years ago, he had had to slip in through a secret passage, but now his position was different.

He was the Saint Disciple Crossweil. When the guards saw he was the Lord's direct guard, they opened the gate for him. Then he headed to the Lord's chambers.

The moment he set foot into the room of rush mats, the heavy scent of the grasses prickled his nose.

"I'm back," he said.

The owner of the room greeted him with nothing but breathing— while peacefully asleep.

"_____"

The silver beast was curled up on the mats, sleeping.

He didn't try to hide his large ears or tail as he slept curled up like a cat. Since Crossweil knew there was a reason behind the slumber, he couldn't easily tell his companion to simply wake.

"Seeing you sleep so peacefully annoys me for some reason, though," he said.

"_____"

"So, Yunmelngen, it turns out it is difficult. We can't alleviate the fear that's taken hold of people that easily. Even after a decade."

In the last ten years, the Imperials still feared the Grand Witch Nebulis and detested the witches who were with her. They were unable to forget the capital being burned to ash.

And then there were also those who took advantage of that.

"The Eight Great Elders. Oh, I guess they're the Eight Great Apostles now."

The people running the Imperial assembly were still alive and well. They continued to have a great influence on the governing body even now, in fact.

Lord Yunmelngen didn't show his face to people. As he couldn't garner trust from his vassals, the Eight Great Apostles continued to have control over the Empire's authorities.

"Also, Yunmelngen, I think there's a meaning behind these past ten years," he told the unresponsive Lord. Crossweil looked at one of his swords. "The astral swords. We've finally forged them, just like you wanted. It seems even the Astrals can't make anything greater than this. But with it, we can..."

He hesitated. In that split second, the silence was suddenly disrupted...

*　　*　　*

…by the sound of an alarm that filled the Lord's chambers.

"……Ugh. What is that?"

It wasn't coming from Castle Tower Seat.

If it had been, then the chamber's automatic alarm would have sounded as well. So that meant it was outside. An alarm was ringing somewhere in the capital.

…I don't like that noise.

…I never wanted to hear it again.

It was the third time he'd heard it in his life. The first was when the astral powers had erupted from the excavation site, the Planet's Navel. The second was when the capital had been engulfed by a sea of flames. And now this time.

Because the two past incidents had been so extreme, he felt a sense of foreboding at the sound ringing throughout the capital.

"I'm going out," he said. "I sincerely hope that you won't be woken by anything."

Then he left the still slumbering Lord.

Crossweil quickly exited the Lord's chambers.

2

He felt a sense of déjà vu.

Yes. He felt a faint chill ever since hearing the sound at the Lord's residence.

A siren kept sounding. His heart thumped faster and faster as he headed outside. The sight that greeted him was black smoke fuming so vigorously it blackened the skies.

The capital was on fire. Though he didn't want them to come

back, he recalled painful memories from ten years ago. Only one ward could have been on fire but seeing the flames and black smoke flickering between the buildings, one couldn't help but think of the witch.

"She couldn't be?!"

He was doubtful. She had left the Empire a decade ago and built her own nation. What point would there be in attacking the Empire now?

"…Please tell me that my intuition is off. Please!"

The larger roads were filled with citizens attempting to escape. The trauma from ten years ago still persisted. Whether they liked it or not, flames in the capital brought about the image of the Grand Witch Nebulis.

"Guh…move aside!"

Crossweil headed in the opposite direction of where the citizens were running. He passed through gaps in the crowd as he ran toward the fires. His voice cracked unintentionally as he saw what was ahead.

He saw Imperial tanks overturned like they were planks of wood. The armed Imperial soldiers were on the ground like fallen dominos. The buildings were half demolished. It was the same as ten years ago.

The Empire's streets were destroyed, and the Imperial forces were devasted.

Above him…

…he saw Eve Sophi Nebulis wearing a black cloak.

It had been a decade since he'd last seen her. She looked the same as back then, still a petite girl. Because she had fused with the astral power in her, time had almost stopped for her body.

"I shouldn't question it when I get a bad feeling about something. I'm usually right."

The streets were silent. The soldiers had been cast aside, and the citizens had all evacuated.

"Long time no see, Eve."

It was just the two of them. Crossweil called her by her name like he always had.

"Crow, your hair's longer." She descended to the ground.

They faced each other, with only a few meters between them... then he noticed something. Eve's eyes were bright red and swollen. She seemed to have been crying. The dust and smoke had mixed into her tears before they had even dried, so it looked almost as though Eve were crying tears of black.

He couldn't help but worry. Even so, there was something else he needed to ask first.

"Eve, what are you doing?"

He looked around again at the destruction.

...The capital's finally recovering.

...The Imperials' hearts are finally healing.

It was all for nothing. Just the very thought of the Grand Witch Nebulis would likely worsen the persecution that witches faced.

"I thought you weren't ever coming back here, after you and Alice—"

"Alice is gone."

He didn't understand what she meant.

...Alice is gone?

...What is Eve saying? They're supposed to be living with each other.

They had run away from the Empire together. They had established a new nation, the Nebulis Sovereignty. He hadn't seen how things were there, but he knew that the first Nebulis queen had to have been one of his sisters, so he'd been sure they would be fine.

He had assumed the two were doing well.

In that case, why were his sister's eyes red and swollen? Why could he see tear tracks on her face?

"…"

He felt his heart squeeze.

For a moment, a sense of foreboding flashed through his mind. The chill he had felt from the third alarm wasn't from Eve's attack.

"…It can't be…"

"It was the wound inflicted by the soldier ten years ago." She wiped her eyes. "Even after she became queen, the injury still troubled her. Then it got worse. My astral power was laughably useless."

"…Ngh."

He couldn't get any words out. It was so sudden that though he understood what she was saying, the emotions hadn't caught up with him.

…*So that's what happened.*

…*That's why Eve is here.*

Her beloved little sister had been taken from her. And an Imperial bullet had done that. So, she had come back to the Empire to get her revenge. As the Grand Witch Nebulis.

"Does it matter anymore? Step aside, Crow."

"…Tell me something first." Crossweil quietly spoke as Eve eyed the Imperial streets.

"Did Alice ask you for revenge?"

"…What?"

"Perhaps it's different. I just got that sense after you told me that Alice was queen."

The Nebulis Sovereignty's queen had been the younger twin.

Since then and until now, the Empire and the Sovereignty hadn't been in an all-out war.

…If she had wanted a war, she could have started one.

…She was even shot by a soldier.

But none had occurred. He was sure Alicerose must have stopped one from ever occurring.

"Crow." Eve's voice was stifled as though she were holding back her rage. "This is about how I feel. I will take revenge on the Empire because that's what *I* want. What's so wrong with that?"

"Right. Then let me say what I want, too. Give me time."

"…Time?"

"The Lord and I are changing the Empire."

"Crow! Are you still obsessing over that dream?!" she yelled. Her bloodshot eyes opened wide as though she couldn't believe it. "It's been ten years! Nothing has changed at all!"

"That's right. We haven't had enough time. A decade hasn't been enough to stem the tide of hate."

It hadn't been enough time for astral mages to forget their persecution at the hands of the Empire. Nor for the Imperials to forget the destruction of the Grand Witch.

"You said nothing's changed, Eve? No. In the past ten years, Yunmelngen and I have been desperately looking for something."

Eve did not ask what it was. To her it was likely nonsense. She had already made up her mind.

"Enough. Out of the way."

She artlessly waved her hand. Using her astral power, wind began to form and was blowing him to the side. He could immediately tell that she was holding back for his sake.

Then he cut through the wind with his black blade.

*　　*　　*

"Wha?!"

The Grand Witch froze, her hand still raised up. He hadn't *just* cut through the wind. The moment he had struck with the blade, the astral power itself disappeared.

"You can intervene with astral power? Crow, what is that?"

"It's hope," he replied.

The black blade gleamed like obsidian. Eve likely saw it wasn't a simple steel blade.

"We didn't waste the last ten years. Yunmelngen and I haven't changed the Empire yet. But we found hope that we'll be able to. We might be able to defeat the calamity at the planet's core with this."

"Huh?"

"Once we do that, the astral powers on the surface should return to the core, too. You must understand what this means, Eve!"

He was sure he could get through to her. She was the person with the strongest astral power, after all. These astral swords could become the hope that Alicerose had been praying for.

"Then the astral powers in the astral mages will also—"

"Stop!" Her shout echoed around the deserted buildings. "Look, Crow...I'm...I'm Alice's older sister!"

Eve almost sounded as though she were weeping. She must have cried enough for her entire life when she lost her sister, but more tears were welling in her eyes.

"Back when Alice was shot right in front of me, and even now with Alice gone. Are you saying I should wait all on my own for a future that may never come to pass?!"

"..."

"You think the source of this is at the core of the planet? I'll fight that thing as much as you'd like, but first I need to deal with the Empire. Until I destroy it, I can't move forward!"

...*Splish.*

A droplet fell onto the dry asphalt and burst.

"Move, Crow!"

"No, I can't!"

The blockhead!

He knew somewhere within him that this would happen at some point. Ever since one of them had stayed in the Empire, and the other had left. He had been prepared for it.

This, the maelstrom of fate that was tearing the planet apart.

The siblings who loved each other clashed.

But before they could watch the fight, Sisbell Lou Nebulis IX's Illumination power disappeared.

EPILOGUE 1

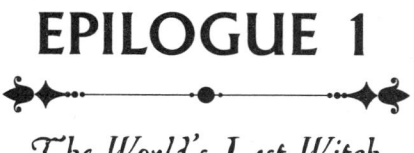

The World's Last Witch

1

The silence was nearly painful to the ears. Not a single person dared say anything. The underground space filled with tension that made everyone unconsciously hold their breaths.

Sisbell was the first to disturb the quiet by letting out a sigh as she knelt on the ground.

"…Ah…uh…haah……I need a short break…the Illumination power has its limit re-creating such a long series of events…!"

Sisbell placed a hand on her chest and took a deep breath. The astral crest that glittered below her fingertips flickered intensely with her breathing.

"Thank you. That was a wonderful power, Princess Sisbell." Risya clapped her back. "Your Excellency, should we continue?"

"No. I've seen more than enough of what I needed. I'm satisfied."

The beastperson's tail swished. Their ferocious fangs were hidden behind their lips.

"Ah, I'm glad. So it really was the Eight Great Apostles. They set the capital on fire. Now I can pass judgment on them freely. And there you have it, Successor of the Black Steel."

"Uh." Iska had unconsciously straightened himself.

Successor of the Black Steel. He knew that meant him, and he had also been aware the Lord and Eight Great Apostles had called him that. However...

It was only then that he realized the heaviness of that title.

"My teacher never told me anything about this."

"Crow's been becoming more and more reticent the last hundred years. According to him, he parted ways with his sister after a 'fight.'"

Iska hadn't known anything at all. He didn't know his master had astral power, nor that he had clashed with his sister, the Founder Nebulis, to protect the Empire.

...But it all connects.

...That's why the Founder was surprised by my astral swords.

It had happened on the outskirts of the neutral city, Ain. When the Founder had first been awakened, she seemed to have an unusual sense of attachment to his swords.

"I haven't seen those weapons for quite some time."

"Those cannot be used by anyone except Crossweil. He baffles me. Why would he entrust the astral swords to a common foot soldier?"

Now he understood why she had found them familiar.

She meant that it was her second time fighting against them. And the second time the Founder Nebulis had fought with a swordsman who held the astral swords. However, Iska still didn't know the details of how the swords came into being.

...This is a story about my teacher and the Founder.

...We can defeat the calamity at the planet's core. But what was the calamity...?

His master had called that hope. It was the hope of the girl named Alice, one of the world's first witches and the younger sister of the Founder. It was a way of making the first Nebulis queen's wish a reality—a queen who had misgivings about the all-out war with the Empire until her death.

That was what these astral swords were.

"Ugh, come on..." Iska put his hand to his temple and let out a long sigh. "Why does he always leave out the most important details?!"

"Um, Iska...?" Commander Mismis hesitantly addressed him. "So Alicerose, the really pretty girl in Miss Sisbell's astral power recreation...she was the first Nebulis Sovereignty queen? And she was called Alice?"

"......Yes. I think so."

"I think I recall a certain princess who has the same name and looks exactly like her, but maybe that's just my imagin—eek?!" She was cut off.

Roar!

When the ground below their feet rumbled, everyone in the underground hall readied themselves.

The ground heaved, and the ceiling lights above flickered intensely. It continued to shake dreadfully, and the disturbance didn't seem to be temporary. It went on for dozens of seconds and showed no sign of abating.

"Wh-what is this?!" Sisbell yelled as she crawled on all fours. "W-we didn't make the Revered Founder's attacks into reality because we watched her past, did we?!"

"This is too big for it to be that." Jhin looked up at the ceiling. "Regardless of whether it's the Founder or the astral corps, they'd attack on the surface. This shaking is coming from below."

"B-but, Jhin! We're two thousand meters below ground," Sisbell shouted. "What could possibly be below us?!"

"The Planet's Navel." Lord Yunmelngen had spoken. Though they were speaking to themselves, their utterance sharply echoed through the hall even as the roar continued.

"You saw it, Princess Sisbell. The excavation site of astral energy from a hundred years ago that reached five thousand meters below the surface."

"B-but wasn't that hole filled?!"

"By the Imperial assembly."

"…Huh?"

"At present, the underground Imperial assembly is established over the cave that was once called the Planet's Navel a century ago."

The rumbling continued. Lord Yunmelngen looked down upon the power that was coming into existence far below them and narrowed his eyes to a needlelike width.

"It's the lair of the Eight Great Apostles. Now, I wonder what's happened?"

2

The Imperial assembly.

Also known as the Unseen Intent.

Its name originated from the diet building having never been noted on any map. The location was only passed through word of mouth from superiors to their underlings, and was never to be written down.

Five thousand meters underground, the deepest part of the Empire.

In the past, it had been an excavation site known as the Planet's Navel.

Within the assembly hall, bright-red alarm lights were flashing.

It had never been broken into before. The only means of entry was the central military base's elevator. And a witch had brazenly entered the Imperial military base.

"All communications have been cut off from the central base."

"Break in through the front... No, they've been destroyed... Not a single person from the communications team has survived?"

Seven monitors showed images of men and women.

They were the same sages who had served the previous Lord. Or, to be more precise, they were the cyberbrains of those people.

A century ago, the octet had sought astral energy, and now they had the goal of obtaining a power that transcended astral power from the planet's core. Though they had lost Luclezeus and now only numbered seven.

"Unbelievable..."

"Was it you, Elletear?"

Ah-ha. The sound of a charming laugh resounded through the space. Her voice, as alluring and kind as a goddess's, and beguiling as a devil's reached them.

"Ah-ha...ah-ha-ha...what a wonderful feeling."

The witch with emerald hair made her way down from the

assembly's ceiling. She passed though the steel walls almost like a ghost. A witch with the face of a goddess had descended before them, performing acts that should have been impossible for a human.

She turned to the Eight Great Apostles.

She wore a black wedding dress...

...instead of typical Nebulis Sovereignty garb. Her dress was like black mist. Though more of her skin was exposed than not by the design of the dress, seeing her only brought on a spine-chilling emptiness.

"You've changed your clothes, is that so?"

"Yes. I thought this was much more witchlike."

She nodded and blushed. She sounded strangely happy, and her eyes looked soft.

"Hee-hee. Ah-ha-ha...I'm so sorry, Eight Great Apostles. It seems the calamity which you seek took a liking to my body."

"Elletear, or rather Subject E, just as Kelvina feared, we found elements within you that would allow you to accommodate the power that slumbers within the core of the planet."

"So you have obtained the ultimate power of this planet."

Only a small number knew the truth. In the core of the planet, there slumbered a calamity that transcended the astral powers. The Eight Great Apostles had yearned to have the power for themselves. Though the Lord and Founder had encountered it a hundred years prior, they had not been able to handle it. As a result, one had changed in appearance and the other had lost her sense of self.

"I believe you said this in the past. That if you were to obtain the power, you wanted to become a true witch. That you wanted to become the greatest and only witch—the last one in the world."

"Yes."

"You also said you wished to reform the Sovereignty. To make it a place where one's worth wasn't determined by the astral crest they were born with and turn it into a true utopia where all astral mages are equal."

"Yes. So, to begin—"

She spread her arms wide.

She arched backward, as if emphasizing her chest. Her voice rung out with excitement she could not hide…

"The Eight Great Apostles are now a hindrance to me."

"_____"

"What did you say?"

"Oh, I'm sure you were aware." She cackled under her breath. "Now that I've assimilated fully with it, none of you are able to compete with me. That was why you ordered Kelvina to take care of me before it could happen. You even took my younger sister hostage to use as a last resort. You believed I couldn't touch you as long as you did that."

All of their plans had ended in failure. From Kelvina's research facility to Elletear's escape. Even Sisbell, who had been captured, had been saved by Unit 907.

"I will of course uphold my promise. I will destroy the Lord, the Empire, the Founder, and the Sovereignty. In fact, I will remake everything beautifully."

She spoke of destruction through her beguiling lips.

"Good night, you fools who sought power."

EPILOGUE 2

The First Siblings in the World

Imperial territory, border checkpoint.

Dozens of cars were lined up and stopped in front of the entry checkpoint.

The station separated the Empire from the outside world. The Imperial forces were permanently stationed in the location, as was a large astral energy detector.

The detector was currently blaring in a way it never had before, continually warning of a powerful witch's approach. It continued for ten seconds… Then for minutes… Yet there was no sign of any Imperial soldiers rushing to the machine.

"So they've withdrawn. The best decision they could have made."

The safety inspection area was up in flames. A man in black watched, looking up at the crumbling walls as he muttered to himself.

The Black Steel Gladiator, Crossweil. He was the former first seat of the Saint Disciples, Iska's teacher, and the former possessor of the astral swords. He walked ahead toward a depression about ten meters wide.

"She's in a bad mood after being woken up. She hasn't changed in the last hundred years."

The cavity was the aftermath of a direct missile, sent by a lone witch in place of a greeting. Faced with her power, the permanently stationed forces had no choice but to retreat.

That had been the right choice. Had they faced her with all the weapons and personnel they had on hand, they still would not have been a match for her.

"She's the strongest and most barbaric woman in the world, after all. I'd actually rather not see her, either. I'm far from perfect condition. And even if that weren't the case...huh!"

His eyes opened wide. His heart sunk in his chest. Crossweil gritted his teeth as he felt a sensation like the very marrow in his bones were burning from the inside out.

"Tsk...this is why..."

The incidents of rejection were starting to get worse. The astral power in his body feared the thing that was awakening within the planet's core. That was what Yunmelngen had told him.

"The Eight Great Apostles..." They were the supreme authority who ruled the Empire behind the scenes. "They've seen the condition I'm in and think that stuff is still wonderful..."

It had happened a century ago. The Planet's Navel had released two things from its eruption. One was astral power. The other was a calamity that had slept in the planet's core. That was what they sought, an astral power that would transcend astral power itself.

"After seeing me...they still think that calamity is the ideal power to have?"

It wasn't something that could be controlled. Yunmelngen's transformation had resulted from making contact with that calamity and being unable to adapt, resulting in rejection. He hadn't realized it until after finding the astral swords.

No astral mage could fight against the Great Planetary Calamity in the planet's core. He was no exception. Even with the astral swords, he had realized he couldn't have done it as long as he was the wielder of the swords.

That was why…

In order to fight the calamity, he had searched for a person who wasn't an astral mage.

He had continued on in his search ever since his sister Alicerose's death and his fight with Eve.

"Iska."

That idiot disciple. Did Iska still remember what he had told him?

"Iska, you're the last of the candidates I brought with me. I'll be direct, you are…"

"Y-yes, master?!"

"You had the least potential."

"You could stand to be a little less direct!"

"You were the most similar to me. That's why I thought you had the least potential."

But partway through, he changed his mind.

If he were to choose a successor, he had wondered who Alicerose would have been happiest with. Only Iska had come to mind.

The talent he wanted in his successor was stupidity.

For example….

He needed someone with endless optimism who would genuinely believe it possible for the Empire and Sovereignty to be at peace.

He needed someone so dedicated to maintaining peace that

they would attempt to release an imprisoned witch despite being an Imperial.

"Knock it off, everyone!"
"Please, listen to me. No one wants this war!"

A century ago…

Had an Imperial soldier like Iska been on the battlefield, the future might have been different. Instead of pointing guns at them, perhaps he would have offered a hand. That was why he had picked Iska.

…I'm sure you'd be smiling, Alice.

…That there's still someone like him in the Empire. Even you would feel reassured if it's him.

It made him want to make that bet. It made him want to entrust his swords to this Imperial.

"Don't you forget, Iska. Your enemy isn't the astral mages or the Sovereignty. Your true enemy to challenge is—"

There was something that couldn't be defeated without the astral swords. In this planet's core.

"That's why this is my role here."

He looked up at the sky. In the all-engulfing, deep blue sky, he saw one black splotch. That was a dark-skinned girl.

"…"

The Founder Nebulis. Her many golden locks of hair fluttered in the wind as she, the sister he had parted from in a fight, looked down upon him.

"You've aged, Crow."

"I prefer 'matured.'"

It had been a hundred years. After fusing with the astral power,

Eve still looked like a young girl. Crossweil's less potent fusion had allowed time to slowly chisel away at him.

"Crow... So you're planning on doing it again." The Founder's eyes glinted with dangerous intent, and her voice was filled with wrath. "Do you plan to stand in my way?"

"I'd like a chat."

"......What?"

She raised an eyebrow. After waiting for some time, Crossweil continued.

"It's been a while since we've spoken. What do you say we have a nice brother-sister chat, without anyone getting in our way?"

Afterword

"…I'm not a good older sister."

Thank you for picking up the eleventh volume of *Our Last Crusade or the Rise of a New World* (*Last Crusade*)!

Finally, Sisbell's Illumination power shows its true abilities. Though Sisbell has been put in unfortunate circumstances again and again, such as being caught by the Hydra and taken hostage at an Imperial research institute, it just shows how feared she is by multiple people.

Through replaying the events of the past with her Illumination power, the main character becomes someone else other than Iska in this volume. Now, as for who it could be…only those who read the book can decide.

As the Lord says, things were decided a century ago.

And it is because a girl and a boy decided to give everything they had to avert this horrible fate—despite taking different paths to accomplish this—that the events of *Last Crusade* could come to pass.

The story is finally in its second half.

I hope you'll continue to watch how the people of a hundred years past and present progress down their paths!

▼Regarding *Last Crusade*'s TV anime

How was the anime broadcast?

This was my first anime adaptation, so it's been a great three months, in all aspects.

To all those who were involved in the anime and to those who watched, I'd like to take this opportunity to say thank you. Thank you so much!

And it seems all three anime Blu-ray and DVDs had a wonderful reception.

I worked hard on the special short stories. For example, the "Forbidden Chapter Founder" story included in the first Blu-ray and DVD is Alice and Iska's fight written from the Founder's perspective. I wrote this story so it would be worthwhile after finishing this volume.

It covers the conflict in Eve, the one who becomes known as the Founder.

I hope you'll take a peek at it.

I will, of course, continue to work hard on *Last Crusade* in 2021 as well!

Well then, I have one more piece of news now.

I have another new series this year that I hope you'll enjoy reading alongside *Last Crusade*!

▼MF Bunko J *Gods' Games We Play* next volume!

A fantasy battle of the wits of humanity versus the gods.

Humanity must win ten games against the gods to achieve

victory. In the history of mankind, no one has yet to clear them all. In this tale, a young man takes up the impossible challenge.

The second volume is coming out May 25th (Tuesday)!

That's actually just a week after the eleventh volume of *Last Crusade* comes out. If you buy both *Last Crusade* Volume 11 and *Gods' Games We Play* Volume 2, then you can get a special short story collaboration! Please take a look at the cover band of *Last Crusade* Volume 11 for more information.

For those who haven't read it yet, nothing would make me happier than if you'd take the opportunity to!

And so, the afterword has come to an end.

Ao Nekonabe, thank you so much for drawing a wonderful depiction of the Lord!

To my editors O and S, thank you for all you've done for the anime and the novel manuscript from day to day. I hope you'll continue assisting me for the rest of *Last Crusade*!

Next is *Last Crusade* Volume 12.

The Empire, Sovereignty, Founder, Black Steel Gladiator, and Lord reunite with Iska and Alice in a battlefield of discordant ideals. And there, the two see...

Well then, MF Bunko J *Gods' Games We Play* Volume 2 is coming out May 25th (that's soon!).

In the fall, *Last Crusade* Volume 12 will be out.

I hope we'll meet each other again then.

On a warm day in spring,

Sazane Kei

※ Finally, I'd like to say thank you for the fan letters.

To M, who sent me a letter last year, thank you for your impressions of *Last Crusade*, *World Record*, *World Enemy*, and *Why Me*, as well as for the bath salts, steam eye mask, and other gifts.

I didn't see a return address for the letter, so I'm very sorry for not sending a response last year. I still use and hold dear the gifts you sent me!

Next Volume

So, Alice.

I wonder, do you have a knight to protect you?

The Empire, Sovereignty, Lord, Eight Great Apostles, Saint Disciples, Imperial forces, astral corps, Zoa, Hydra, and all manners of those with power have gathered in a chaotic battlefield where the witch's laughter rings.

When Iska and Alice meet on the battlefield once more, the thing which sleeps in the planet's core awakens.

The twelfth act, a dance between the Supreme Witch and the most powerful swordsman.
It's a trade, Iska.
I will offer you my thorns.

Our Last CRUSADE
OR THE RISE OF A New World

VOLUME 12
Anticipated for Fall of 2023!

HAVE YOU BEEN TURNED ON TO LIGHT NOVELS YET?

86—EIGHTY-SIX, VOL. 1–11

In truth, there is no such thing as a bloodless war. Beyond the fortified walls protecting the eighty-five Republic Sectors lies the "nonexistent" Eighty-Sixth Sector. The young men and women of this forsaken land are branded the Eighty-Six and, stripped of their humanity, pilot "unmanned" weapons into battle...

Manga adaptation available now!

WOLF & PARCHMENT, VOL. 1–6

The young man Col dreams of one day joining the holy clergy and departs on a journey from the bathhouse, Spice and Wolf. Winfiel Kingdom's prince has invited him to help correct the sins of the Church. But as his travels begin, Col discovers in his luggage a young girl with a wolf's ears and tail named Myuri, who stowed away for the ride!

Manga adaptation available now!

SOLO LEVELING, VOL. 1–7

E-rank hunter Jinwoo Sung has no money, no talent, and no prospects to speak of—and apparently, no luck, either! When he enters a hidden double dungeon one fateful day, he's abandoned by his party and left to die at the hands of some of the most horrific monsters he's ever encountered.

Comic adaptation available now!